The Border Police

THE
BORDER
POLICE

One Hundred and Twenty-Five Years of Policing in Windsor

Written by C. H. Gervais

Researched by Mary E. Baruth and G. Mark Walsh

Penumbra Press

Gervais, C. H. (Charles Henry), 1946-
   The border police

ISBN 0-921254-50-4

1. Police - Ontario - Windsor - History.
I. Baruth, Mary E. II. Walsh, G. Mark (Gregory Mark).
I. Title.

HV8160.W56G47 1992   363.20971332   C92-095447-2

Acknowledgements

The author would like to acknowledge the help of other sources: The *Evening Record,* the *Windsor Star, Windsor This Month,* the vast array of city bylaws and police commission minutes from Windsor's Municipal Archives at the Windsor Public Library, as well as information culled from the Windsor Police Service Museum.

Thanks must also go to the following: the staff at the *Windsor Star Library,* especially Deborah Jessop, Chief Librarian.; to Bill Bishop, photo editor, Bev Mackenzie and others in the photo department at *The Windsor Star* for providing the painstaking task of re-photographing and printing most of the photographs for this book; John Nash who supplied priceless photographs of his grandfather Abe Nash; Carl Morgan, former editor at the *Windsor Star* for help on the events surrounding one of the largest robberies in Windsor; my father, Ted Gervais, for taking me on a tour of old Ford City and its environs to give me a sense of what it looked like back in the 1920s when he first came to live here; Ray Renaud, for background on his father, Claude Renaud, police chief from 1936-1950; Susan Gervais, the granddaughter of James Wilkinson, whose name figures highly in this book and in the history of the Windsor Police; Larry Kulisek, professor at the University of Windsor, who provided details on the investigation into the police department in the 1950s; to Judge Gordon Stewart, former police commission member, for the broad view of what law and order was like in this community; to former police chiefs, Carl Farrow, John Williamson, and Jack Shuttleworth; Marjorie Preston, widow of Chief Gordon Preston, Leona Hughes, widow of Chief John Hughes; the staff at the Windsor Police Services, in particular Mary Jane McMullen, Joy Dennis, Mary Solan, Ernie Belanger, Don Mills, Barry Horrobin, Alfred (Alfie) Wells (for supplying photographic work as required); to John Moor of the Windsor Police Association for supplying a wealth of information in its old yearbooks; and to Harry van Vugt and Kris Russelo for their meticulous proofing of these pages; and finally, to my wife, Donna, who, at least, pretended to be patient and understanding throughout the ordeal of the writing.

Special mention must go to the Windsor Police Service for demonstrating unwavering interest in preserving its history. The first positive step in that direction was in 1977 when Chief John Williamson opened the Windsor Police Service Museum. Ten years later, under the direction of Deputy Chief Alec Somerville, the police transferred a large number of its historical records to the Municipal Archives at the Windsor Public Library for safekeeping. The ultimate objective was the creation of a history of the Windsor Police. The main supporters of such a project have been Chief Jim Adkin, Alec Somerville and Superintendent John Burrows. All have promoted actively the writing of such a history. It has been the unflagging enthusiasm of Chief Adkin, that has made this book become a reality. None of this would have been accomplished however without the support of both Mary E. Baruth and Mark Walsh, the two researchers who together presented the initial outline and concept for this project. Their untiring work helped me pull together the disparate strands that make up this lively story of Windsor's police constables. Finally, I need to thank both James Bruce, editor of the *Windsor Star* and Linda Balga, head of Public Relations, for their cooperation and support.

The researchers wish to acknowledge the Parker-Steele Family for unrestricted access to the papers of Alton C. Parker, Debra Evans of the Burton Historical Collection at the Detroit Public Library; Jack Webster of the Metropolitan Toronto Police Museum; John Dirk of the Archives of Ontario; Judy Levesque, registrar at the Francois Baby House Museum; the Long Point Region Conservation Authority, especially the staff at Backus Historical Complex; to Marian Baruth and Charlie Dean; and finally to Elaine Mortimer, secretary to the Windsor Police Services Board.

Contents

This book is dedicated to
the memory of
Alton C. Parker
Canada's first black detective,
a man who personified
the best of Windsor's finest

PART ONE

Lawbreakers and Bylaw Makers
Policing in the 19th Century leading up to
and
after Confederation

Police Department badges from various municipalities 1934-1935. Windsor Police Service.

1
Early Years and the Question of Authority

The thought of a community stretched along an international border with only a handful – indeed, only three or four men – enforcing the law seems inconceivable today. That, however, was Windsor in the mid-19th century as it struggled to its feet to become a city.

The clapboard homes and the muddy streets may not have cut a pretty sight to a visitor, and in some ways, may not have seemed worthy of defense. Still, there was a fierce loyalty and pride among residents on the south shore of the Detroit – they did not intend to relinquish or give themselves over to their American neighbors.

One wonders, however, at how such a society could have managed with a scruffy band of law enforcers chosen, not so much for their abilities, but their size. The old "Police, Charity and Health committee" minutes from the 1800s report a demand to hire "three suitably big men" to handle lawbreakers.

The laws being broken then were those against drunkenness, assaults, bootlegging, quarrelling, fighting, gambling. Not exactly big time crime. Yet, Canadians were aware of such crimes. The famed Reno Gang, for example, prominent among U.S. outlaws, retreated to Windsor in 1868 after robbing $96,000 worth of gold and bonds en route to the U.S. treasury. Five members of that gang fled to the safety of Windsor. They chose Windsor, partly because it was across the border, but also because Charlie Anderson, their safecracker, had lived here.

In Windsor, crimes committed were more against the person, not the institutions. There seemed more of a respect for authority, institutions, even its police constables. For that reason, there was little trouble enforcing the law. There was also little demand for training. Police constables then were "night watchmen," not policemen.

Even though there may have been this veritable respect and truculent sense of fidelity to institutions and authority, ironically, there was an air of reckless abandon among the population. It was not uncommon for even the most distinguished persons in the community being brought up on charges. A doctor from the asylum was convicted of drunkenness. Police constables themselves were hauled into court for intoxication and neglect of their duties.

While there may have been robberies, in most cases, these centred

Gibbet Iron

around a desperate need for food. Bank and train robberies were rare. Most of the charges laid were for "craziness," resorting to insulting and abusive language, driving a team of horses faster than allowed by the law, bathing nude in the Detroit River, or even against bakeries for baking bread of insufficient weight. So significant was this latter bylaw that the chief constable for Windsor kept a scale on his desk to weigh bread suspected of being below standards.

While there was profound regard for the state – perhaps a reflection of their British roots – it seems bewildering that this huddle of river towns would throw their trust to just a few men, especially considering how untrained, and ill-equipped they were, moreover because there were genuine threats of invasion from the Fenians in the 1860s. True enough, residents banded together, forming a militia, arming them-selves with everything from pitchforks, axes and clubs to shotguns, pistols and scythes. They lit bonfires along the river front, and awaited the invasion they believed would set their homes ablaze, and turn their lives into turmoil.

Earlier, during the Civil War, there was some concern of an invasion. Even so, there was no rush to arm the population. There wasn't a move to establish a full-time police force.

Then, as some writers have pointed out, what dominated people's attitude more was a distinct respect for authority. The priority wasn't a strength in numbers. In time, this utter regard for authority was the *Canadian* way of doing things. June Callwood in *Portrait of Canada* relates the story of a single mountie riding into Sitting Bull's hostile camp a few days after the Battle of Little Big Horn, and spotting several fresh American scalps and horses with U.S. cavalry brands. He boldly advised Sitting Bull to obey Canadian laws, or he would "deport the whole tribe," and Sitting Bull nodded. It was done with sheer authority, not at gun point, not with a backup of soldiers.

This respect for institutions, law and order, and jurisdiction was so strong, Callwood wrote, that during the Klondike gold rush of the 1890s, it was not unusual for a miner to leave behind his gold in an unlocked cabin. Across the border, ruthless Yankee dilettantes battled it out in the streets with little or no regard for property.

In some ways, Windsor, and the border towns of Walkerville and Sandwich, differed little from their counterparts across the country. Just as American miners rushing north of California were stopped short by a British judge and soldiers warning that the gallows would be their fate if they used their weapons, so were visitors to the river towns along the Detroit River met with a righteous attitude. In Sandwich, for example, it was the indomitable William Hands, sheriff of the district, who rode about on a white horse and ruled with uncompromising justice. In the

Sketch of the William Hands' house ca. 1900. Artist Miss. H.V. Bowlby. Municipal Archives-Windsor Public Library.

early 19th century, the law was clear. As a matter of fact, it was posted right on the iron cages, or bilboes, swinging from gibbets at the junctions in Sandwich. These cages held the rotting corpses of criminals. The accompanying warning read: "Murderers, horse and sheep thieves shall be hung in some public thoroughfare and remain in full view of passersby until the flesh rot from their bodies."

Jean Barr, a local historian in 1904, in a paper read to the Ontario Historical Society in Windsor, maintained that justice was dealt with "a liberal hand." There wasn't the slightest hesitation at hanging a thief. It didn't stop there. Barr said even the innocent were "terrorized and made miserable by the warnings of justice." Of course, this came in the form of these ghastly bilboes that sent a shudder through the communities.

The smell and the sight of these rotting corpses were so offensive that townspeople voiced their opposition. Few dared to remove the bodies.

Story has it, according to Barr, that Hands, "a man of courage and decision," may have sympathized with those complaining about the gibbets holding two Chatham men, and secretly removed them himself. Several years later the bodies were discovered by someone excavating a nearby property for a gravel pit.

Indeed, Windsor was a unique place in this time, offering a comfortable way of life for both law-abiders and lawbreakers. The two seemed to coexist easily, without harassment. People may have broken the law here, but still held an unwavering respect for authority that extended even to events across the international boundary. There certainly were

Southern sympathizers in Canada, but mostly people harbored a deep sense that things had gone awry in the U.S., and that there had to be a return to authority, to fairness.

As an example, during the Civil War, people reacted to the death of Abraham Lincoln in much the same way that later generations would mourn the assassination of John F. Kennedy. Alexander Bartlet – for years Windsor's town clerk, and later its police magistrate – wrote in his diary April 15, 1865, that when he rose that morning he could hear newspaper boys on the street announcing the death of Lincoln. He promptly went down to the town offices and hoisted the Union Jack at half mast. He wrote, "Almost every shop and store in Detroit was draped in black and all closed," Ten days later, he joined the council and some 50,000 people in Detroit in a march to mourn the death of the American president.

Bartlet also reacted to the Fenian invasion, not so much with fear, but indignation that people had such a disregard for what others held to be important. Namely, one's livelihood, or way of life. He called these Irish agitators, "troublesome scoundrels and ruffians." He complained bitterly, "Is it not contemptible that a set of cutthroats can actually plan to invade a peaceable country?"

Interesting, too, during this time was the development of Canada's first secret police. It was formed by Gilbert McMicken, the Englishman who is regarded as the founder of the present day Royal Canadian Mounted Police. He had come to Canada in 1832 to be a customs collector at Queenston, and later served as a county warden, a member of the Legislative Assembly from Welland, then a banker.

As a friend of John A. Macdonald (later Canada's first prime minister) McMicken was asked to set up the Western Frontier Constabulary. It was formed to combat the practice of "crimping" where brokers resorted to kidnapping potential recruits for the American forces during the Civil War. They did this in order to detour the bounty being offered to Canadians to enlist. The money would wind up in the pockets of the brokers, rather than in those of the recruits.

McMicken's job was to track down such abuses. He sent trained men into the border towns to spy on such activities. The copy of the Special Orders given to his network of spies read: "You will observe and watch parties known as 'Scalpers,' 'Bounty Jumpers,' 'Substitute Brokers,' whose calling it is to entice soldiers to desert from her Majesty's service and to entice them and other of the people to enlist in the army of the U.S."

Bartlet referred to McMicken in his diaries, telling how Windsor's local constabulary assisted in arrests. Such action on the part of McMicken's force was born out of a sense of duty, for it was against

British law for any British subject to serve in a foreign army. McMicken's men, however, also guarded against possible invasions from the Fenians.

What is interesting about this special force was that it went about its espionage without being armed. One spy wrote to McMicken, who was directing all of his activities from Windsor, that he thought he might be more effectual if armed with at least a revolver. McMicken turned down the request. Again, not so surprising, considering the early stories of the Mounted Police, where the very presence of an officer was enough to impress.

2
The Police Constable

The development and establishment of police forces didn't come about in any abrupt way. Rather, it evolved as society needed constables "to preserve the peace." In the early days of Upper Canada, or for that matter, any other part of British North America, the term "constable" was common, not "police." According to Philip C. Stenning in *Legal Status of Police* the word "police" does not appear until well into the late 18th century. Even then, the term held a different meaning, referring to, as Dr. Johnson states in his dictionary, "the regulation and government of a city or country so far as regards the inhabitants."

It wasn't until 1849 with the passing of the Baldwin Act, establishing elected local government in all municipalities that "police" activities are mentioned. Section 81 stipulated that town councils could pass bylaws "for establishing and regulating a Police for such Town." Section 74 indicated there could be in each town "one Chief Constable, and one or more Constables for each Ward of such Town . . ."

By law, the police magistrate in each town had the authority to suspend the chief constable "for any period in his discretion." In the 18th Century, the appointment of constables was left to justices of the peace. The Baldwin Act then transferred this jurisdiction to newly elected municipal councils. And nine years later, the Municipal Institutions of Upper Canada Act permitted the formal establishment of police forces. Under this, constables had "special duties of preserving the peace, preventing robberies and other felonies and misdemeanors, and apprehending offenders. . ."

These pistols originally used by Colonel J. Prince were stolen from the Hiram Walker Museum (François Baby House) and used to break into a car in the early 1970s. They were returned to the museum. Windsor Star, (ws).

3
The First Policemen

Prior to Confederation, policing in Ontario – or Canada West, as it was called then – was undertaken by the Royal Canadian Rifles. In Windsor, they were stationed in the barracks on the site now occupied by City Hall Square. It is likely that their presence was here more for defense on the international border than anything else, especially in light of fears of an invasion by the Fenians.

In terms of actual police work – dealing with bootleggers and gamblers – this was handled by a motley band of men in each of the river towns. In Windsor, Samuel Port was chief constable. His official appointment, however, wasn't made until three months prior to Confederation when Windsor passed Bylaw 98 on April 1, 1867, designating Port as the Chief, and hiring William Brown, Charles Bussette and Henry Goodenough as constables. It would be 1870, before Windsor passed a bylaw (Bylaw 143, Nov. 7, 1870) setting up its police force.

Prior to this, policing was mostly a bylaw enforcement exercise – merely watching over businesses and homes at night. Sandwich had been made the county seat in 1796, and as such, was the place where any prisoners were dispatched, or dealt with by the courts. The authorities of what was then called The Western District allowed the Sandwich officials to move an old block house from Chatham, Ont. to be converted into a jail. Soon after, the building was destroyed by fire, forcing the commanding officer at Fort Malden to let Sandwich use an old vessel in the river as a holding place for prisoners.

A brick Court House and jail was built about 1800 and stood on property now occupied by Mackenzie Hall and the County Jail. It was a square red building surrounded by a palisade of cedar posts. Alexander Mackenzie, Canada's second prime minister, was responsible for building Mackenzie Hall in 1855. Windsor, too, had a jail, or a "lock up," installed at its town hall offices, large enough to hold two prisoners. And when Sam Port was the Chief, he was forced to cram six prisoners into the cell.

As the *Border Cities Star* reported:

To protest…the prisoners started kicking the end of the building in unison. It took only a few seconds to uncover the fact that the building could stand very little kicking. In fact, the boards started to loosen with the first boot. It took less than five minutes to kick the end right out of the building and the prisoners were on their way again.

Sam Port captured most of the kickers, but a couple left town rather than face the ire of the husky blacksmith.

The force in Windsor – if it can be called that – had its problems in those years, both before Confederation and following it. Sam Port in essence was "a one man police force" for many years. He would deputize constables when he needed them, but for the most part managed on his own, even continuing his blacksmith business in the village. Port rarely walked a beat, or involved himself in a crisis, unless pressed into it, and then he'd pin a badge to his coat and run off to investigate.

Port seemed embroiled in one controversy after another. It was common during the 1850s to hold prize fights in some outlying areas, even though it was illegal. In 1858, two Detroit boxers battled it out in an outdoor ring near Windsor, but not within its boundaries. Port was there, along with a deputized constable, Thomas Mason. They both stood and watched the fight, but took no action to arrest the organizers, or the boxers. Samuel Smith Macdonnell, who had been elected mayor that year, and had been the reeve of the village of Windsor from 1854 to 1857, was infuriated at the behavior of his policemen, and threatened them with suspension.

Port took his job seriously, yet sometimes his decisions didn't sit well with the town's council. Bartlet's diary of Feb. 3, 1868, demonstrates this: "The mayor (James Dougall) came down on Sam Port like a thousand ton of bricks and gave him fits for appointing the night constable without authority." Apparently, Port had taken it upon himself to designate the night watchman, thereby contradicting council.

In those days, too, council assumed a more active role in policing. Bartlet himself, Town Clerk for a 20 year period (1858-1878), wrote in July 1868, how he was wakened by Constable Brown "to go and see the body of a man that was brought in by the night ferrymen." Years later when Bartlet was police magistrate, he earned money on the side – $24.65 one month – for cleaning out the police cells.

The force hardly grew over the next few years. Once more, the town resorted to hiring night watchmen. It also expanded the duties of its constables. Goodenough, an Episcopalian, was appointed a "day constable" by the police committee in 1870. He also acted as an assistant licence inspector and "health officer." For these extra duties, he would be paid 50 cents a day. The force hired Henry Mitchell, too, as a night watchman to accompany Bussette.

In 1870, Windsor pressed ahead to formalize its police department. It realized that the present force did not give "satisfaction to the public that is deemed necessary for its safety and protection."

To that end, it passed Bylaw 143, Nov. 7, 1870 stipulating that the force consist of a chief constable, one day constable, two constables as night

Windsor Police Department, 1889. From left, (first row), J.Langlois, A. Nash, D. Grieves, (second row, seated) W. Giles, C. Mahoney, F. Hess, A. Griffith, (third row, standing) W. Lester, G. Livingston, M. Meston, J. Jackson. Windsor Police Association.

watchmen and ward constables.

The bylaw outlined the duties of the chief constable as taking charge of "the Lock-up" in the Town Hall, as well as employing whatever measures necessary to prosecute offenders.

The council demanded that instruction, or training of constables, would be left to the chief constable. It was left to him to acquaint himself, as well as his men, with the town's bylaws and Ontario's statutes. The chief constable's salary was set at $400 a year. Individual constables earned $1 a day.

In the bylaw, signed by Donald Cameron, a dry goods store owner and both police committee chairman and mayor until 1874, a "Code of Rules" was called for by the police. Those rules and regulations, however, didn't come into use until 1876. And it appears from what

Bylaw 143 created the Windsor Police Department in 1870. Municipal Archives- Windsor Public Library.

occurred in Windsor at that time, such rules were needed badly.

By 1871, it appears the system wasn't working too well. A police committee report in November described the Windsor force as in disarray. Cameron wrote: "There is a great want of harmony of action amongst them. Some are more busily engaged watching the movements of the other than serving the town." Some constables were "making the tavern their headquarters and passing their time at such places instead of attending to their duties as constables."

Cameron recommended disbanding the present force, and replacing it with one consisting of a chief constable and three constables. The emphasis in this committee report, too, was upon hiring only "thoroughly reliable men who will perform their duty without fear." He also proposed an increase in pay.

There is an emphasis, too, in this report on sprucing up the "look" of the force. Cameron asked that belts and overcoats be supplied to the force.

Disbanding of the Windsor Police Force didn't occur until three months later. William Bains, employed by the Great Western Railway, was appointed chief constable. Henry Mitchell, James Crawley and Thomas Hillar were named his subordinates. The committee's minutes, ushering in these changes in the force, show it wasn't prepared to bring in a Code of Rules. It requested "further time to report." The committee had hoped something would be provided by "provincial authorities."

In March 1872, Cameron was still advocating a Code of Rules, but wasn't getting anywhere. Members of the force were quitting, and being replaced with temporaries. Two years later, there was more trouble. The reality was that the police department was plagued with serious problems of conduct. Once more Cameron, as mayor, tried to regain authority over the force. In yet another bylaw, No. 217, passed June 15, 1874, the council seized "control of the police force of this town." Up until then, the Board of Commissioners – the mayor, the judge of the county court, and the police magistrate – had jurisdiction over the police.

In time, the new chief constable proved to be a problem. Bains complained that private watchmen, hired by merchants in the town, were passing themselves off as policemen. He cited one man as interfering with "the due execution of the duties of the regular force." Besides, Bains maintained, this man was often "in a state of intoxication and totally unfit for his duties."

Bains impressed upon the Commissioners the necessity of having all private watchmen investigated before being appointed, so that the police might check out "their characters and capabilities" to ensure they were "trustworthy and capable men." He warned that if they violated the rules of the police force, they should be discharged immediately.

Bains also demanded an investigation into the conduct of one constable for taking visitors into the cells to see the prisoners without the chief constable's consent. This officer was criticized for not making arrests when ordered by the chief. Apparently, this same officer advised some prisoners to lay charges against Bains for "false imprisonment." Bains claimed that some constables were accepting drinks "for the purpose of getting a prostitute out of the Lock-up."

About this time, too, there were complaints leveled against Bains by two men arrested at the Davenport House. They were placed in the Lock-up and suffered "other indignities there."

A year later, Bains was at the centre of controversy again, this time for being "neglectful" in not arresting a man who had robbed the Montreal Bank in St. Catharines. Bains apparently had been tipped off as to the robber's whereabouts, but didn't arrest him. The police committee took no action because the man who leveled the charges against Bains failed to show up for the hearing.

Bains continued to be a problem. In fact, he was asked to resign twice but was reinstated both times.

On January 31, 1876 the police committee proposed yet again a new bylaw with "a code of rules." By now, it had became apparent that something was needed to prohibit police from frequenting "saloons or taverns" except when requested to break up a disturbance.

In February, 1876 Windsor Town Council under Mayor R. L. McGregor finally passed the bylaw setting out rules of conduct for its police force – only six years after it was demanded by Cameron. These regulations, set out in Bylaw 254, stressed that police officers were not permitted to accept "rewards' from anyone, unless approved by the mayor and council. They also couldn't quit the force without a notice in writing, weren't permitted to go into saloons unless their presence was "actually required to quell a disturbance or otherwise in the execution of (their) duty, and that their pay would be deducted if they were absent from duty because of sickness."

The new code stipulated that each constable would be supplied with "one blue coat, one light, two pairs of trousers, one cap, one instruction book, one baton, one whistle and in addition one great coat and one cap to be supplied every second year, none of which is to be his property at any time, but is merely for his official use when acting as a member of the Force."

So adamant was Town Council about this latter rule that policemen were warned that when they quit the force, any damage to the equipment or clothing would be deducted from their pay.

Windsor's police met with still more trouble in May, 1876. Police Constable Charles Cane was reprimanded by the committee for "absenting himself from duty without notifying the chief of police." He was also accused of "unnecessary cruelty and harshness" when he shot a dog when he was making the arrest of the dog's owner.

That same month, Constable Robert Craig was accused of being drunk while on duty. He went before the police committee and confessed his guilt, and pleaded for reinstatement. The committee complied with this request. But Craig was back again with the same charge some time later. Much later, both he and Joseph Langlois were suspended by Bains for insubordination. Both were reinstated by what was now being called the "Police, Charity and Health Committee." This was in the summer of 1881. Craig was finally fired from the police department – the reason given in the committee minutes as due to "dual suspensions."

Oddly enough, by the spring of 1882, putting control in the hands of the council didn't prove to accomplish anything. The Police, Charity and Health committee complained that the police were still in a state of "inefficiency," and that a solution might be the formation of a Board of Commissioners, consisting of none other than the mayor, the county court judge and the police magistrate.

Windsor was a rowdy, wild place in those late years of the 19th century. Saloons were open seven days a week. The community had leapt from a stagecoach hamlet and a village, to a town, then a city. In the 1830s, Windsor's population hovered around 700. By 1892, the population swelled to more than 10,000. Throughout that period, the city had become a kind of revolving door for immigrants, runaway slaves, rural people yearning to find a new life in an urban environment – in reality, a place to stop over, to see if life might be better. Hundreds of families paused at this river town, coming in with the arrival of the Canadian Pacific Railway in 1883, pondering the future. Many crossed the border, heading to the Midwest. Others remained here, carving out a new life.

According to the former *Evening Record*, published in the late 19th century in Windsor, the town was also "a safety zone to safe blowers, hold-up men, thieves and vagabonds." The newspaper goes on to say that "crooks of all dyes congregated here. They hatched plans for jobs, sped away to execute them in the store holds of wealth in Detroit and then hurried back to recuperate from their 'banking' labors in 'quiet little Windsor' . . .Brawls were frequent, sharp knives appeared before sharp words had time to echo."

Early handcuffs. Windsor Police Service Museum.

Charlton & Company's General Directory of 1875-76 described Windsor as having a "pleasant, clean and healthy appearance," and a place where many took up residence for "the summer season." It is clear, however, that the view here was that of a community of working people. They are praised for "their sterling industry and perseverance." American visitors, according to Charlton's directory, were taken aback by Windsor's children. So much so that they sarcastically describe how these "sweet little cherubs . . . pack the sidewalks, and amuse passers-by with unearthly yells and showers of mud."

Windsor was not unlike any other enterprising Canadian town, stated the writer: it had "a town hall, a common council, hotels, barber shops, billiard tables, and an extensive brigade of bootblacks (who stand around the ferry docks and fight 'fur dat job.')

But its physical appearance was far from picaresque. The town huddled modestly along the shoreline. Ouellette Avenue ended at Park Street. Sandwich Street, or what is now Riverside Drive, was not paved, and each spring it was almost impassable. *The Border Cities Star* recounted how the street was regularly engulfed by buggies and drays.

The first conviction of Rebecca King, 16 October 1861, for disorderly conduct and exposing her person in the streets. Municipal Archives-Windsor Public Library.

On one occasion, a frustrated citizen hitched his team to a boat and drove it down the street "in mute protest for the eyes of the councillors."

The biggest advancements it seems at the time in Windsor was not so much the growth in industry, which included such manufacturers of brooms, leather and wooden ware, wine, vinegar, soap, candles, boots, shoes, and carriages, but the numbering of the houses, and the lighting of streets after dark.

It wasn't a pretty place; it was a working-class town. There wasn't a gentry, as such, although a handful of citizens described themselves as "gentlemen" in the 1864 census records. Most were carpenters, cabinet makers, bartenders, grocers, blacksmiths, boarding house owners, tinsmiths, tailors, masons, sailors, or railway men working on the Great Western Railway. Most homes were wooden and modest. The community was often beset by fires. So frequent were they that one night after a blaze, Alexander Bartlet reported that while attending a fire committee meeting yet another fire started up.

Bartlet's diary provides a vivid and colorful picture of that era. In terms of crime, most offences were those involving what people did to other people, or to themselves: stashing a seven-month-old fetus at the back of a saloon, reckless driving of horse-drawn carriages, petty thievery, drunkenness. But people could be charged with swearing, or as one man was in 1865, for carrying a restricted weapon, a bowie knife.

One name that continually crops up in court records is Rebecca King. She was charged in October 1861 for exposing herself in the streets and fined $5, as well as court costs of $3.10. This became a usual occurrence. She was possibly the most common offender, her name appearing on a conviction of exposing herself, stealing, being drunk, and using offensive language. She rarely paid her fines, and usually spent time behind bars, in some cases doing what was termed "hard labor." Many of the offenses took place in connection with taverns, or saloons. She was sentenced for 10 to 21 days at a time. In one instance, in June 1871, she was charged with using abusive language and vagrancy and was put in Sandwich Gaol for two months to do "hard labor."

Women were actually among the majority convicted of using insulting and abusive language in the public streets, probably because it was unacceptable for women to speak in that fashion.

In July 1862 five men – Robert Sutton, William Hutton, John Clark, Robert Hutton and John Francombe – were charged with bathing and indecently exposing themselves in the Detroit River. Not all crimes seemed that serious by today's standards. A Philip Langley in May 1863 was fined $3.50 for destroying and damaging rhubarb plants.

Then again, in those early years, one finds records of sexual assaults on children, with offenders being sentenced to "hard labor" in jail.

Liquor offences were the most common. These included being drunk on any day of the week, selling liquor without a licence, but especially for selling it on a Sunday. The law took liberties, too, charging a man with "lying in the street and appearing sick or drunk."

Even the most influential, including policemen and firemen, broke the liquor laws. Bartlet speaks about a fire one winter night in December 1868 when one of the firemen was drunk before going to the fire and all the next day. It didn't help that during the fire itself, that "they (helpers) took round the whiskey in basketfuls."

In those latter years of the 19th century, although the police force had grown, the town still balked at spending more on enforcement. In March 1890 Alexander Bartlet and Town Clerk Stephen Lusted both complained that the single telephone line in the town hall was sadly insufficient. Recommendations called for another line, especially one for Chief Constable William Bains. It was finally installed. A year later, the police force also acquired a typewriter – somewhat of an advancement since the machine had only been invented in the late 19th century. The force also acquired a stenographer, a move that came about because of yet another dismissal due to the previous clerk failing to take down evidence in an orderly fashion.

From this period of the late 19th century, the names of a few heroes surface in spite of the controversy surrounding a small force. One such man was Joseph Langlois. Although he had been disciplined by the police commission for insubordination, he was a tough-minded law officer who served 45 years on the force. Earning $37.50 a month when he started in 1872, he worked 15 hours a day. In those days, the police also received "fees" for taking prisoners to jail.

Newspapers of that period reported the heroism of Langlois, especially an incident where he rescued a woman and her two children from being burned to death in the Opera House on Sandwich Street. Attempts had been made to save the three, but rescuers gave up. When Langlois arrived on the scene, he didn't hesitate to climb a ladder to the second floor that was engulfed in flames. He discovered the three huddled in fear, and led them quickly to an open window and down the ladder to safety. Hundreds of onlookers cheered.

Langlois also battled the infamous five-member Siddell Gang. On one occasion, the gang was about to toss the body of one of its victims into the Detroit River when Langlois attempted to tackle one of the gang members. But the officer found himself on his back lying on the ground with a gun pointed at his head. Without giving it a thought, Langlois brushed away the weapon, rolled the man over, and arrested the gang member. Moments later Langlois chased down a second member, and arrested him.

Joseph Langlois was considered one of the toughest fighters on the six-man force. Once a gang attacked him and beat him nearly unconscious. As the 1954 souvenir edition of the *Windsor Star* reported, "his mouth was so badly battered he couldn't eat for three days but he still made his rounds . . . Within a week he had rounded up the three men most responsible for the attack and had them behind bars."

Another good "fighter" was Seraphim Maitre, who started with the Windsor Police in December 1894. Described by the papers as being "afraid of no man," he was rated one of the strongest men in the country. Maitre is best remembered, however, for a confrontation with the heavyweight boxing champion Jack Johnston. This was toward the end of Maitre's service with the Windsor Police. Being only a few steps from retirement didn't hamper the five-foot nine officer from going after Johnston. The boxer had been on a cross-country tour of Canada, and was heading for Detroit when Maitre stopped him.

Police in London, Ont., had wired ahead to Windsor to have Johnston held at the border till he paid his speeding fines. Maitre stationed himself at the Ferry Dock, and when he spotted Johnston, he stood on the gangplank to block his path.

As the papers reported:

> The huge heavyweight, who had licked all opposition, tried threats at first. He told Maitre he would use his influence to get him busted off the force but still Maitre stood his ground.
>
> Then Johnston tried bullying tactics. He told Maitre he'd be sorry the

Constable Joseph Langlois. Windsor Police Service Museum.

C. Mahoney, 1889
Windsor Police Association

next day when he regained consciousness and remembered he had run up against the world champion.

Maitre didn't budge an inch. In fact, he told Johnston to come ahead and try his luck. When the champion hesitated, Maitre laid out in plain language what he could do and what he couldn't when driving in Canada."

Johnston backed down and returned to the Windsor Police Station handcuffed by the much-smaller Maitre. The fighter agreed to pay the fines in London, as well as those incurred elsewhere in Ontario.

In another instance, Maitre went to arrest J. R. Crittenden for some minor offence, and ran into the Siddell Gang brothers – Sam, Aaron and John – who had decided to prevent the officer from carrying out his duty. The *Evening Record* recorded it thus: "Maitre stood up against the four as long as he could. At last they got him down and in the melee his nose was broken. But he got his prisoner and, reinforced, went back for the gang, too."

Another hero was Charles Mahoney, who was awarded a "gold medallion" for his heroism in assisting a man who had been the subject of an attack. In July 1893 Windsor councillors expressed their approval "to the very courageous manner in which (he) performed his duty in the perilous position in which he was placed . . . in attempting to arrest, alone and unaided, the three desperate characters who had set upon a fellow citizen." In the scuffle, Mahoney narrowly missed being shot. The following September, the constable received the gold medal from the council as a reward for his service.

The Extradition Act came into the force in 1892, and had the effect of cleaning up Windsor a little. Many old gangs retreated across the border, not wishing to find themselves arrested and sent back to lawmakers in the U.S.

4
The Billygoat-Bearded Police Magistrate

The name that dominates the late and second half of the 19th century in Windsor is the billygoat-bearded Alexander Bartlet. A gentleman and pioneer. And a man whose name is linked to just about every facet of Windsor's history – business, education, religion, municipal affairs and law. Bartlet had been secretary to the school board for 34 years, helped found the first Presbyterian church in the city, and served as the town's clerk for 20, its magistrate for 30. He was a meticulous record keeper. His diaries that survive reveal how involved and keen he was about his community. Bartlet never failed to take the opportunity to run out to a

Alexander Bartlet in front of his Chatham Street home. ws.

fire in the middle of the night, or to attend to the plight of someone down-and-out who might prevail upon the town for food, or shelter. During the Fenian scare, he freely billeted soldiers in his house, a sprawling two-story frame building at the corner of Ferry and Chatham streets in a location now occupied by The Old Fish Market restaurant. Bartlet was famous for his own detective work, diligently investigating deaths in the community to determine if they were accidental, or intentional. He speaks of these in his diaries, indicating how he took roads in the early spring that were "truly appalling... and appeared to me to have no bottom" in order to examine the body of a man who had died of excessive drinking.

Bartlet was born Dec. 31, 1822 in Scotland. He came to Canada, settling first in Amherstburg in 1841. He arrived at the age of 18, with two brothers – James and William – and took up the trade of carpentry. At that time, the Essex peninsula was largely wilderness with great areas of uncut forests. In later years, when he no longer made his living from woodworking, he would write in his diary how much he enjoyed using a new buck saw to cut wood.

Bartlet moved to Windsor in 1853. Five years later, he was appointed its town clerk by Macdonnell, the first mayor following incorporation of the town. In 1859 he was named secretary of the Board of Education. He was devoted to that job. Often he'd tour the schools, occasionally filling in for teachers, and offering assistance in grammar lessons. He'd cross the Detroit River to shop at bookstores, returning with an excellent Latin text for Windsor students.

Bartlet was a deeply religious man, who helped found St. Andrew's Presbyterian Church. The first was a mission church across the street on

Alexander Bartlet, Police
Magistrate. ws

Victoria, just near his house. Later the church relocated to Park and Victoria, where it still stands. In those days, Bartlet's involvement included being superintendent of the Sunday School, and occasionally when there wasn't a clergyman, he'd take to the pulpit himself. Bartlet also appreciated good music, and made it a practice to carry a portable organ from his home to the church. Another member of his family would play it.

In 1879, Bartlet was appointed police magistrate, and retained that office until he was 86. But old age didn't deter his ability. As a writer in a retrospective piece much later wrote for the *Border Cities Star*, it was difficult putting anything past him when he presided in the courtroom: "So shrewd is the aged magistrate that no matter how attorneys try to befog the issue, almost never is a case reversed on Alexander Bartlet."

The newspaper writer goes on to describe him as having "original methods," pointing out how his deep involvement and interest in the community gave him an edge in the courtroom. Often Bartlet would recognize "family histories, down to the second cousins." The journalist wrote:

A man is up for wife-beating. Testimony is conflicting. Is the man jealous or was he merely drunk and ugly? Ten to one that Bartlet knows the fellow since childhood but in case it's necessary, the magistrate will slip quietly out and find a trustworthy witness. What sort of temper has the accused? Was he always jealous? That settles it, he acted according to his disposition. He must be severely punished.

"What's this? Tom Jones up for larceny. I knew him 40 years ago when he was a schoolboy. He was always a bad egg; petty thievery; now something serious. The man is a born rascal!"

The magistrate, acting on his leading impulse, scolds prisoners. He scolds them soundly, like an indignant Dutch uncle; like an exasperated father. If he is going to let a man off, that man first receives a lecture, more dreaded than a term in prison. The prisoner's ears will burn for days.

Bartlet also had his own way of dealing with drifters, who appeared on this side of the river from Detroit. He didn't throw them in jail, or impose a heavy fine on them. He knew full well they wouldn't be able to raise the money. And so he would trick them. He'd ask these drifters, if he let them out for a few hours, would it be possible for them to raise enough to pay the fines. "Could you get it if I let you out for an hour or so?" Bartlet would inquire. Naturally, the hoboes would agree to the offer. But as they stepped from the courtroom, Bartlet made sure someone slipped them a ferry ticket.

It was said that Windsor became a haven for criminals fleeing the justice system in the U.S., and while they remained here, they behaved.

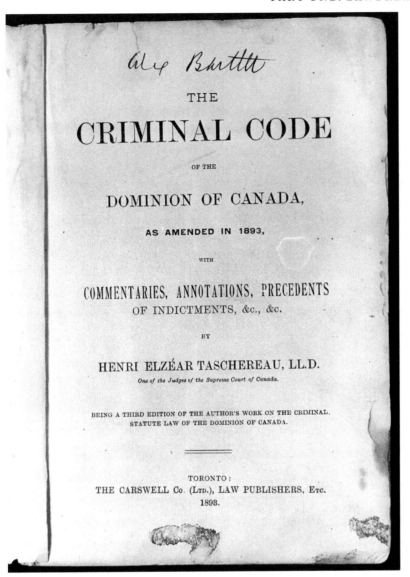

Alf Bartlett

THE

CRIMINAL CODE

OF THE

DOMINION OF CANADA,

AS AMENDED IN 1893,

WITH

COMMENTARIES, ANNOTATIONS, PRECEDENTS

OF INDICTMENTS, &c., &c.

BY

HENRI ELZÉAR TASCHEREAU, LL.D.

One of the Judges of the Supreme Court of Canada.

BEING A THIRD EDITION OF THE AUTHOR'S WORK ON THE CRIMINAL
STATUTE LAW OF THE DOMINION OF CANADA.

TORONTO:
THE CARSWELL Co. (LTD.), LAW PUBLISHERS, ETC.
1893.

Bartlet's copy of the Criminal Code.
Municipal Archives-Windsor
Public Library.

The reason lay with Bartlet's resolute Christian faith that wouldn't tolerate crime. One newspaperman at the time of Bartlet's death in 1910 said, he was known as "the grand old man" of Windsor, and what marked him above others, was that "he lived his beliefs." This was certainly true in the courtroom where he ruled with an iron fist. He made it clear to the police that they had to carry out their duties with authority and discipline. Although these officers occasionally erred themselves, they still managed to keep Bartlet's court filled with offenders. The *Border Cities Star*, in reflecting on Bartlet years later, maintained it was not at all unusual to have more than 90 cases on the court docket in the Division Court.

5
Bylaws & Public Morality

List of licences issued by Windsor in 1892. Municipal Archives of Windsor

This eclectic and odd mix of religious cultures – Methodism, Presbyterianism and Roman Catholicism – collectively accounted for the high-brow morality that seemed to dominate Windsor. Its lawmakers busily drew up bylaws to keep public morals on the right course. One of the first all-encompassing public morals bylaw was Bylaw 112 "The Regulation of Public Morals," passed in March 1868. It reflected an earlier law, approved in August 1859, but went further. It is ironic that now more than a hundred years later, the ancestors of these pioneer families would go to great lengths to reverse many of these laws. Namely, the bylaw enforcing the "due observance of the Sabbath," stipulating that no store owner, or proprietor of any business, could conduct business on that day.

Covered under this bylaw was an edict against distributing or posting "indecent placards, writings or pictures." There were laws drawn up prohibiting "houses of ill-fame" (brothels), forbidding people from gambling, being drunk, or swearing, or from exposing themselves, or bathing in the Detroit River. A revision of that bylaw in July 1870 enlarged upon these laws, and stated that charges would be laid against those giving, or selling liquor to children. That new bylaw – Number 254 – issued in Feb. 14, 1876— set out a code of conduct for the police force itself.

On occasion, lawbreakers got a break. Allan L. McCrae in "Border Cities Recollections" in the *Border Cities Star,* recalled how a prominent hotel proprietor and his bartender were both summoned to appear before Judge Caron by a whiskey informer, known all over Canada as "Whiskey Mason." The hotel owner was charged with selling liquor on Sunday and during prohibited hours, in contravention of the statutes of Ontario.

Judge Horne, then a practicing barrister, appeared for the defendants, both of whom swore positively that no liquor had been sold over the bar during the previous Sunday or at any other time during prohibited hours. Because "Whiskey Mason" had no other evidence to produce other than his own sworn statement, Judge Caron dismissed the case.

As was the custom in those days after the court had adjourned, Judge Horne, Judge Caron, Mr. Alexander Bartlet, and one or two others, adjourned to Judge Caron's private apartment in the old town hall.

McCrae then describes the revelation that followed:

The judge (Caron), after lighting his long, old-fashioned clay pipe, remarked in a rather reminiscent tone of voice, "It is an extraordinary thing to me how some people will perjure themselves for the sake of a small fine of twenty-five or fifty dollars." Of course Judge Horne inquired, "Why, judge, do you mean to say that my clients perjured themselves?" "Well," replied Judge Caron, "you may call it a lie, if you choose, but when a man kisses the book and calls God to be his witness that he will tell the truth, the whole truth, and nothing but the truth, and I know all the time that he is telling a lie, I call it perjury. You heard both that the hotel proprietor and his bartender swear positively that no liquor had been sold over the bar on Sunday. I was there myself and had my drink of brandy, for which I paid ten cents, as I do every Sunday after mass and before I go home to dinner."

Sometimes municipal bylaws failed to cover other practices considered immoral. Even so, the message of disapproval was registered clearly. This was the case when Lillian Langtry, known as "Jersey Lily," crossed the river to perform at the Opera House, Windsor's first theatre, then a part of the Davis Block. Langtry had been barred from a Detroit auditorium, and thought she'd bring her show to Windsor. The *Border Cities Star* remarked how "Detroit theatergoers were more discriminating and insisted on keeping their morals unimpaired." Lillian met with a stern demeanor on the part of residents here. She fled the scene, declaring how "terrible" she found residents on the south side of the Detroit River.

Morality wasn't the only thing covered by the municipality's bylaws. Other laws addressed the practice of driving teams of horses on Windsor's streets, or prohibiting someone from driving cattle into the downtown. There were regulations that banned "spitting on sidewalks and other pubic places." That bylaw – No. 1114 in 1904 – stated that someone found guilty of spitting on stairways, passageways, at the entrance to a building used by the public, or on the floor of any room, hall, building, or in any place that was employed by the public, would be subject to a $10 fine. There were laws, too, regarding the emissions of smoke, the quality of bread and the inspection of milk by the town's sanitary inspector. That inspector would analyze the milk for its butterfat content, and would set forth the name of the vendor and the comparative quality and value of samples taken.

The enforcement of these bylaws was the responsibility of the police and the courts. As the city grew, this became increasingly difficult. Many old bylaws from the turn of the century were still in force at the time of the First World War. Such laws were regulated by the chief. In most cases this meant issuing licences. These even included newsboys. By the First World War, there were 200 licences taken out for the sale of the *Evening*

Bylaw enforcement included the prevention of animals running at large. ws.

Record and the *Border Cities Star.*

Stephen Lusted's name is found on many of the bylaws before the First World War. He was the town clerk, appointed to that position in 1880. The English-born man, who had been in the newspaper business before going into municipal affairs, arrived in Windsor in 1865. He worked on the *Windsor Record and Journal*, then belonging to P.G. Laurie. When Laurie sold out, Lusted established *The Windsor Record*, and published it until 1880 when he took the job with the Town of Windsor.

PART TWO

Growth of the Border Cities, The Automobile, Prohibition, Amalgamation 1900 – 1935

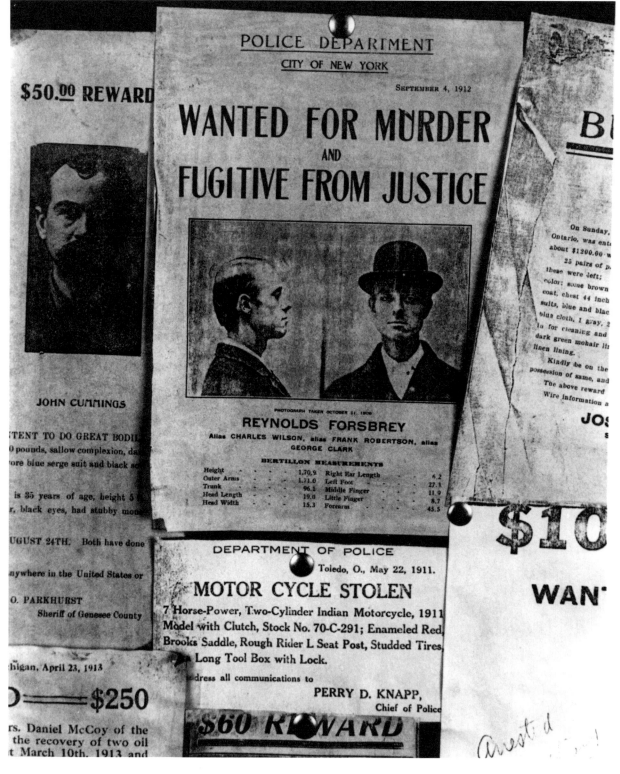

An example of a wanted poster. Windsor Police Service Museum.

1
A Hard-boiled Constable

At the turn of the century, Windsor was still very much a rough-and-tumble community, and the police still faced the challenges that came with it. They were in constant demand, often just mediating fights. Even with what one might consider the most tame situation – like an election – the police force was called in. Election days were chaotic and volatile. The *Evening Record* reported that "It was one big round of fighting, drunken men from early morning until sunset. To arrest every man merely caught fighting on those days would have meant filling the coup with all the qualified electors of the city."

Although the police collected special fees, they were underpaid, worked long hours, and felt unappreciated. Constables felt pressured by a council that wanted a force to protect and regulate its community. The municipality felt it couldn't spend the money to train, or prepare these men for the job. As in the 19th century, it was expected that the chief would provide the training and that the men would be selected for their ruggedness, size.

The product of this system – and the kind of community that was Windsor – produced some notable characters. One such man was hard-boiled, cigar-smoking Abe Nash. Like Langlois, he straddled the turn of the century, starting as a policeman when he was 22 in 1887. As a *Star* writer said of him years later, "He was a genuine hero. Tough, stocky, courageous, but with a touch of human compassion that set him apart from the rest . . . Abe Nash was the kind of cop that kids dreamed of (being), and townsfolk held in awe."

When his son, Claude Nash, donated a medal, along with some handcuffs used by his father, to the Windsor Police in 1975, he said of his father, "You know, my dad was like Sergeant North of the Mounties. He was once a very prominent man in these parts."

Indeed, he was. His heroics included rescuing six drowning boaters on the Detroit River, arresting a notorious robber Sam Jarvis, and tracking down and arresting German sympathizers who attempted to dynamite the Peabody Building and the Windsor Armouries during the First World War.

Nash was born in 1865 in Dundas, Ont. He moved to Sandwich when he was 14, and soon landed a job with the Great Western Railway. In that first year with the Windsor force, he made a daring rescue of six blacks who were at the foot of Ouellette Avenue about to cross the Detroit River in a small boat. The vessel tipped. The *Evening Record* reported the incident:

Abe Nash in early police uniform
with Windsor Police. John Nash
personal collection

Windsor first municipal hall, 1856-1904. It was demolished in 1968 as part of the downtown redevelopment. ws.

Officer Nash, who was on the dock, at once bravely plunged into the river and succeeded in recovering five of the party . . . at the imminent risk of his life . . . Even while Nash was effecting the daring rescue, thoughts of duty were uppermost in his mind for when a thief attempted to steal the clothing of the people he had just snatched from a watery grave the police-man arrested him at the point of his revolver and had the satisfaction of see-ing him convicted and sentenced to a long term in prison . .

Nash was presented with a gold medal by the town, and soon after was promoted to sergeant.

In 1900, he was in the news again for arresting Mark Marshall – one of "Blinky" Morgan's henchmen. Five years later, he demonstrated the sort of toughness and constitution that a police officer needed on the Windsor force, when he arrested Sam Jarvis, or someone newspapers in those days described as a "desperado." Nash caught him robbing a fruit vendor of $100. When he was escorting him back to the station, Jarvis got the best of him. Nash had been wheeling his bicycle with one hand and holding a gun to Jarvis with the other as they approached All Saints' Church.

Abe Nash as a provincial police
officer at South Porcupine, Ontario.
John Nash collection.

The *Evening Record* reported it thus:

Just for an instant I took my eyes off the man. He wheeled like a flash
and plugged me . . . I took after my prisoner, but staggered like a dazed
man. Everything looked black before me. . .

Nash had been shot in the neck with a .38 calibre revolver. But just
when Jarvis thought he'd escape, Joe Langlois was on the scene to help his
partner. He had spotted Jarvis running with a gun in his hand. Langlois
arrested him, but Abe Nash, who had stumbled onto to the pair, wasn't
finished with Jarvis. He told the *Evening Record*, "I kicked him in the head
until he became insensible. I guess it is a good job that I had a pair of rubber
heels on my boots, or his face would have been badly mangled."

Nash left the Windsor Police briefly to take a job in building the
Michigan Central Railway Tunnel in 1910. Eager to get back to police
work, Nash joined the Provincial Police, which had just been formed in
1909. Nash's first posting was in Essex County, and his first week on the
job saw him in a gun battle with horse thieves near Harrow. The tough,

Articles and artifacts pertaining to Abe Nash. Windsor Police Service Museum.

Abraham Nash. ws.

cigar-smoking Nash was transferred to Northern Ontario, where he worked in South Porcupine and Schumaker. There he snowshoed, and used dog teams to get around the bush country. His family remained in Windsor, and Nash wrote hundreds of postcards.

Nash returned to Windsor in the midst of the First World War. He died there in 1916. More than 2,000 attended his funeral.

His grandson, John Nash of Amherstburg, remembers his grand-mother's stories: "I guess in those days Abe was a pretty tough guy . . . Punishment was on the way to the police station, but as grandma said, sometimes he'd come back pretty black and blue, too . . . I guess that was the price you paid."

John Nash remembers his grandmother telling him how Abe Nash couldn't tolerate any deviation from the law: "He used to say, 'You're either innocent or guilty – there ain't no in-between.'"

2

A Scrapper

Another disputatious type from the days at the turn of the century and right up to the First World War was Elias Wills. As the *Evening Record* pointed out, "scrapping was almost the chief qualifications for a job on the force . . . A man did not have to go looking for trouble. If he accepted half the challenges offered he was a busy man."

According to the papers from the turn of the century, Wills, who later became chief constable, "reigned in police circles." He had joined the force in 1883 when Windsor had a population of 6,000. In 1889, he was appointed sergeant, and the force added another man. In 1891, Wills was made acting chief constable. When Chief Constable William Bains died, he was named head of the police department.

It was during those first years on the force that Wills gained the repu-tation as being a rugged, tough confident cop who was fast with his fists. It is said that he actually enjoyed confrontations. His presence on the street stood as a veritable warning to criminals. The solid-looking Wills relished the opportunity to go head to head with anyone challenging his authority.

As chief constable, Wills increased the force to nine men immedi-ately. By the First World War, the force had jumped to 29 members. Wills' own salary at that time was $1,850 annually, while first class constables earned $1,080.

Besides duties as a constable, Wills also acted as a clerk for the police court. This was because Windsor – with the exception of Toronto and Hamilton at that time – had more cases than any other city in the province.

Police Constable Ross ca. 1917 on
Harley Davidson Motorcycle.
Windsor Police Service Museum.

3
Bicycles, Motorcycles and Strikes

Following the First World War, the Windsor Police Force made strides
at modernization, but only in a small way. The earliest references to
motorcycle officers show up in the records in 1917, and as the years go on,
tenders are issued to buy these vehicles for officers. The first officer to
ride these motorcycles was Constable Ross. In 1919, the force purchased
a Harley Davidson from Bowlby and Glunns at a cost of $600. The
following year, the force purchased two more from the same firm at a
cost of $760 U.S. each.

But while funds were being invested there, the force was still using
bicycles after the war, buying them from Eli Parent at a cost of $22.70. In
fact, they were using bicycles right into the 1920s. Lieutenant Alfred
Carter of the detective division in the special 1954 souvenir edition of the
Windsor Star wrote that patrolmen in the 1920s still made their checks
on bicycles. It is ironic that now in the 1990s, bicycles have returned to
the force, and the police are patrolling parks and recreational areas.

Windsor Police Department paddy wagon ca. 1922. Windsor Police Service Museum.

In those days, the "beat cop" would walk 25 to 30 miles during a shift. Carter remembers the outskirts of the city back in 1923 as having very little pavement: "There were times when I walked through mud and mire up to my knees."

It seems that Windsor's police officers – numbering 37 during and immediately following the First World War – contemplated supporting a strike by streetcar drivers in the summer of 1919. The Board of Police Commissioners asked that its secretary draw up "an obligation of loyalty" to be taken by members of the force. The board maintained that "those who did not see fit to sign it," should consider resigning. In fact, the board dealt with the resignation of one officer over that matter.

4

The Automobile and The Mechanical Policeman

Safety and Education

The impact of the automobile on police work really began to be felt at the beginning of the 1920s, as police departments in the Border Cities

Early police wagon, a Gotfredson.
Windsor Police Service Museum.

saw the need to fight the growth of rumrunning. A car to police work meant more than just chasing after criminals. Safety became a priority, and a veritable concern. The automobile on streets, once dominated by pedestrians, horses and bicycles, posed a dramatic contrast, and real problem. Accidents occurred at a rapid rate. Year after year bicyclists were being knocked down by motorists. Children, playing in the streets, were often the victims of cars. In 1924 Chief Daniel Thompson issued a warning to parents in Windsor to keep a closer watch over their children. He placed the blame for accidents, not on the part of the drivers, but upon the children themselves. He said, ". . . upon thorough investigation no blame was attached to the driver (for these accidents) . . . as in many cases it was discovered that the children thoughtlessly, in their play, either ran in front or against the automobile as it passed."

By the late 1920s and early 1930s, the police began their first educational forays into the schools, with the purpose of informing children about safety on the street. In 1931, M. S. Wigle, then chief of the Windsor Police Force, responded to 10 fatal accidents from automobiles by enlisting the resources of the Ontario Safety League and dispatching officers to Windsor schools. He said, "I believe these lectures have been beneficial . . ."

Magistrate W.E. Gundy, Chairman,
Board of Commissioners of Police
1920-1924. Windsor Police Service.

In July 1927, the Ontario Government introduced a ruling that drivers had to be licensed. The move was meant to cut down on the number of accidents. The fact was that by 1922 the automobile was entrenched in the lives of many. An estimated 8,000 automobile owners resided in Windsor and Essex County. According to Neil F. Morrison in his book, *Garden Gateway to Canada*, advertisements then boasted of tires lasting more than 5,000 miles.

Windsor seemed like a natural environment for cars, since it prided itself on having more concrete pavement than any other city its size in North America. Of course, the major automobile plants operated in its environs. Ford was the first to come, and major expansion to its plants took place in the 1920s. By 1928, there were 8,000 men working at its factories out of Ford City, putting out an average of 500 cars daily. General Motors, too, began building motors here as early as 1919. By 1928, there were 575 employed by the operation. The other two automobile companies in operation here were the Studebaker Corporation and Chrysler.

"The Stop Bylaw"

It was during Thompson's tenure that the city first passed a "Stop Bylaw," to regulate traffic. This new bylaw, introducing the city's first stop signs, stipulated that all east-west traffic intersecting Ouellette Avenue from Sandwich Street to Tecumseh Road had to stop before crossing over. Similarly all traffic north and south between Ouellette Avenue and Gladstone Avenue had to stop before making the turn onto Wyandotte Street. Thompson argued in his 1924 report that accidents involving automobiles were finally on the decrease because of the bylaw approved in August 1923. Thompson said the new laws had the effect of decreasing the number of accidents, from 468 in 1923 to 267 in 1924.

The Stop/Go sign ca.1923. Windsor
Police Service Museum.

Ford City followed suit with a similar Stop Bylaw in 1924 for streets intersecting Sandwich and Drouillard, and ordered the first stop signs for the municipality.

Ford also resorted to "a bobbing safety silent policeman," or a device designed to regulate traffic. It was purchased at a cost of $24, and placed at Sandwich and Drouillard in the summer of 1926.

While the car was beginning to dominate, the horse was still a fixture on city streets in the 1920s. Police records indicate that horse drawn carriages crossing the border numbered 20,000 in 1923. By contrast, the car had definitely taken over by then, with 424,870 cars crossing the border into the U.S.

Early Windsor Police Automobile fleet. Windsor Police Service Museum.

Mechanical Fitness

There was a growing concern over the mechanical fitness of cars in the 1920s. In some annual reports, police chiefs complained that motorists weren't heeding warnings about proper braking systems in cars. It seems there were no laws or standards being enforced – the police instead merely waged a campaign against motorists who had defective brakes.

In Chief Constable Mortimer Wigle's annual report in 1929, there was a plea, too, for drivers to pay special attention to "lighting equipment, especially their headlights as defective lights (were) found to be the cause of several accidents." In those days, the lights were not so precise. They had to be adjusted manually for focus.

The Police Flyer

In terms of police work itself, by the 1920s, with Prohibition in full bloom, the car was a paramount feature. From the annual reports, Thompson, and his successors, betrayed their delight over the purchase and use of "The Police Flyer," a sprawling, fast, sleek Studebaker Six reserved for chasing rumrunners, and responding to burglar alarms and holdups. The car was bought in 1921 from Thompson Auto Company for $2,800.

Sergeant Yokum, who later became a detective, was the force's mechanic. He labored over The Flyer for several years, keeping it on the road, thoroughly overhauling it. It was replaced in 1927 by yet another Studebaker.

In 1922, the Windsor force purchased a Reo as a patrol car. This was replaced with a Gotfredson in 1925 which was used as a patrol wagon. The old Reo was converted into a stake body truck. Eventually it was junked. Its parts were removed to be used in an old street sweeper the city operated.

In 1922, Ford City Police bought a Ford touring car. Until then, police actually hired drivers, or took prisoners by taxi, when they were transferring them or making arrests. The automobile the Ford City Police wanted had to be equipped with "an extra tire, speedometer and spot light, with insurance fully covering all liability."

The Ford proved to be less than satisfactory. A few years later, police complained that it wasn't fast enough. Its top speed was 35 mph. According to the Police, Water, Fire and Light Committee report of

Opening day of the Windsor Police Department building, 1921. ws.

April 1924, "a special attachment" that cost $18 increased its speed by another 5 mph, but this was deemed "insufficient . . . to catch speeders."

It appears that Ford Motor Company had a special influence over its namesake town's police department, so that it couldn't buy anything but a Ford. The location of Chrysler Canada in Ford City was in fact the reason the town's name had to be changed. When the first car rolled off the Chrysler Assembly line in 1929, it simply could not be produced in Ford City. Thus, the town was renamed "East Windsor." The East Windsor Police Force's first purchase of a car was a Chrysler in 1929. The department bought a 75 Roadster at $2,195. An trade-in allowance of $495 was given on the Ford.

Lt. Carter in the 1954 souvenir edition of the *Windsor Star* maintained that it was under Chief Thompson that the sergeants were given patrol cars. Sergeant Dan Bordeau and he were the first men in the department to be assigned to "scout car duty."

Carter remembered it as a Model T Ford touring car:

> No one else ever used that car. And it looked like an easier job so we had to work an extra hour . . .There were no windows and it was pretty cold in the winter. . . We rode that 1926 touring car until 1934. It was winter and we had Mayor Dave Croll and the late Assistant Crown Attorney Louis St. Pierre go for a ride with us. They found out what we were going through. The next police commission meeting resulted in buying 1934 models. Even then we had no heaters in the cars.

Insurance

The police in Windsor in the early days of the automobile showed compassion for drivers, and publicly advised pressure upon insurance companies. In the 1922 annual report, Chief Constable Thompson recommended stiff laws to curb car thefts. He said this might lead to "favorable consideration" on the part of insurance companies.

Signal Lights

In the summer of 1925, Windsor became the first city of its size on the North American continent to introduce traffic signal lights. The traffic control system, installed downtown, replaced four officers, and cost the city $8,000. But its implementation caused a furor of complaints and fears. There was fear over an increase in jaywalking, as well as concern for the safety of children who relied upon "the big policeman" to help them across the street, and of course, there was fear over whether or not motorists might understand the new system. It seems incomprehensible now that motorists wouldn't be able to grasp a system of lights – amber, red and green – something that we take for granted today, but at that time it was a concern. Ald. Tuson, traffic Commissioner, was frustrated himself in having to explain its use to cynical bystanders at council. *The Border Cities Star* reported that the persistent question being asked by motorists was how the system worked.

Tuson put it simply almost as he had been talking to primary school children today: "There are three lights, amber, red and green. The amber light is not a 'go' signal. It is simply a warning to motorists who are waiting for the change in lights that the change will take place in five seconds . . . The whole thing is simple. Stop with both the amber and red light and go with the green."

Still, some aldermen wondered if the public would grasp the subtleties of this new system.

The newspaper also dubbed these freestanding towers as "mechanical policemen," underlining the fact that they replaced the human dimension in the downtown. It had not seemed all that long before that Constable Mortimer S. Wigle had been assigned the job as traffic cop at the intersection of Ouellette Avenue and Sandwich Street (now Riverside Drive). Elias Wills, chief Constable in 1914, had recognized the need to direct traffic downtown because of the increase in automobile traffic to the race tracks, and appointed Wigle to the job.

Council argued that the increase in automobile traffic had necessitated this new electrical system. Ten years before, car traffic from the

At the corner of Park and Ouellette
ca. 1925. WS.

ferry brought about 100 cars a day. In 1925 this had increased to 1,600. The *Border Cities Star* revealed, "Even scientists and engineers are being called in by the police departments of the world to assist in solving what has been admitted by police heads in all the big cities as the greatest problem now confronting them. And so the human traffic officer in Windsor must take a back seat to be replaced by a system of 'silent policemen.'"

Six months later, Chief Constable Daniel Thompson observed that while the lights indeed were working "efficiently," there was still a need for traffic cops in the downtown area. "The fact that the signal system is comparatively new and will, of necessity, have to be tested in many ways before we can come to any measure of success . . ."

Although it was promised that the new system would be in operation 24 hours a day, in fact, it wasn't always the case. A few years later, after three fatalities at Ouellette and Wyandotte, the chief constable in his 1929 report wrote: "As these accidents happened at night after the traffic lights were turned off, it is a question as to whether the operation of the lights at this intersection, would have prevented these accidents."

Chief Constable Daniel Thompson,
1921-1928. Windsor Police Service.

5
Parking Cards

It had been Chief Constable Wills at the beginning of the First World War who foresaw the problem posed by automobiles. In the Twenties, it only got worse. For the first time, Windsor began talking about "parking problems." Chief Constable Mortimer Wigle in his 1929 annual report cited downtown congestion as due to more office buildings going up on Ouellette Avenue. He wrote, "I would suggest that the businessmen and their employees find parking space in parking lots, garages etc., and leave the available street space for their customers. When shoppers find it difficult and sometimes impossible to park in order to do their shopping downtown, they do business elsewhere."

It was a problem even earlier. Chief Constable Thompson introduced the first "parking tickets," then called "parking cards." He introduced a system of "marking cars." With both measures in place, it was possible for the Windsor Police to collect $1,887 in fines. Thompson pointed out in his 1926 annual report, however, that the amount could have been greatly increased had officers tagged out-of-town automobiles. "I felt it was unfair to tourists and especially strangers in the city to be fined for minor parking offences." He also said the police took "responsibility and the opportunity in those cases to give a warning to the said offenders."

6
Renegade Chief

Daniel Thompson was chief for seven years, and during his tenure the Windsor Police began to advance, including the construction of a new police station, development of the identification bureau and introduction of parking violation tickets, and a system of mechanical traffic lights.

Yet those seven years suddenly came crashing down upon him when it was determined he was involved in mysterious money dealings.

It seemed the pug-face, belligerent and garrulous Thompson was at the centre of controversy throughout his leadership. Early on there were charges leveled against him. Among those were that he protected "a disorderly house" on Dougall Avenue. Such charges failed to take hold, and Ald. Mitchell, who had made them, was forced out of public life for one year. As the *Border Cities Star* indicated, in the next election, residents showed their displeasure with Thompson, and returned Mitchell to council at the head of the polls by a large majority.

The next attack came in the fall of 1922 by a committee of council, led primarily by Mayor A. W. Jackson. This attack centred upon Constable Albert MacCaulley who was accused of brutally assaulting a handcuffed prisoner. Although three witnessed the assault, the charges were dismissed by the police commission.

Robert Ballantyne, later elected to council on a "police clean-up campaign," complained about MacCaulley, but in respect to different assault.

At the time of this investigation, there were calls for a Royal Commission to investigate the Windsor Police Force. Pressure had mounted steadily from all quarters, most notably by the *Border Cities Star*. In October 1922, Presbyterian clergyman D. N. Morden, addressing his congregation, praised the newspaper for its campaign against immorality. He said the war against the purveyors of debauchery had shaken "the sink-holes of iniquity."

The most devastating attack on Thompson, however, came in the fall of 1927 when Windsor City Council demanded his resignation for complicated money dealings that saw funds being diverted to the police chief. Ald. Clyde W. Curry's tenacious demands paved the way for Thompson's debacle. It also led to drafting a resolution, passed by a vote of 7 to 5, that stated that the public had "lost confidence in the administration of justice in the city." City aldermen decided the only way to rectify the situation would be to fire the chief and reorganize the department.

The motion, put forth by Ald. Garnet A. Edwards, and seconded by Curry, was supported by Ald. Charles Tuson, who had been mayor of the city from 1917 to 1918.

Tuson spoke eloquently in favor of "the way of getting rid of those who have been responsible for the lax enforcement of the laws." He argued strongly for a new police force, and declared that he believed both police commission and force had "fallen down badly."

The *Border Cities Star* praised Tuson's speech, describing it as "the finest . . . ever heard at Windsor City Hall. Tuson told council, "During the last few years we have been trying to promote industry, a bridge, a tunnel and other projects to help build up this wonderful district in which we live . . . but mothers and fathers are not going to consider (moving) . . . to a city with the reputation this city has today."

He said, "It is time to dispense with these cheap, rotten bootlegging and gambling joints, or we could never again raise our heads . . . Are we to become a red-light city?"

Ald. Edwards confessed that Thompson had made "threats" against him, and other aldermen. Apparently, the glib chief had warned he'd "get" them one by one. Edwards maintained, too, that the chief had forced Inspector Mortimer Wigle to give up $100 from a sum of $500 which the inspector had been granted by council to go to the police chiefs convention in Vancouver. When Wigle refused to agree to the arrangement, Sergeant Wilkinson was instructed to hand $100 over to Thompson and charge the funds to rental of the chief's summer cottage for 18 days.

Chief Thompson was charged with having made false returns covering up large sums running into thousands of dollars that went into either his pocket or those of his officers.

The Windsor Police Commission launched its investigation, which took on the proportions of a trial, and lasted into November. Thompson finally resigned Nov. 19, 1927. He made the announcement a half hour before the Commission released its decision. It had come after a long drawn out hearing that rocked the city, and demonstrated just how wide open Windsor had become, as well as how deeply the police department had fallen in esteem. Day after day at those hearings, witnesses had stepped forward to supply damaging evidence against Thompson. Curry's own charges were the lengthiest and most detailed, maintaining that the chief had openly permitted gambling in some two dozen locations along Sandwich, Pitt and Ouellette. He also contended that Thompson siphoned off money for advertising that was supposed to have been spent on the police convention banquet held in Windsor. Curry also accused the chief of police of collecting licence fees from local race tracks, and clubs that were intended for licences with the city, but never passed these funds on to authorities.

Curry was not alone in his criticism of Thompson. Witnesses turned out in droves to testify against him. One woman declared she paid the chief protection money in order to keep a blind pig in operation. A Pitt Street barber told the enquiry that he spotted two policemen "directing traffic" into the premises at 14 Pitt Street East, a well-known blind pig operated by Ross Fleury.

At times, the seriousness of the charges produced a rather sobering and sombre effect. One afternoon, Sergeant James H. Wilkinson, head of the identification bureau for the force, revealed the contents of a telephone call from some "enterprising Detroit gunmen looking for a job" who offered to help:

> I was sitting in my office in the police building when the telephone rang. A voice said, "Is that Windsor?" And I said, "Yes." They asked who was talking. I told them, and the voice at the other end of the wire went on, "Say, do you want that guy Curry bumped off?" I said, "What do you mean?" and they said, "Do you want him bumped off – taken for a long ride?" I said, no, we didn't do that sort of thing in Canada, and they hung up."

It didn't help Thompson that he had been quoted several times as threatening those aldermen.

Thompson left in disgrace. He had come to Windsor in 1920 after having served as chief of the Peterborough Police. His first police job, however, had been with the London Police where he had been a patrolman in 1893. In 1905 he resigned to go into private business, and a year later became chief of the Woodstock force. Four years later, Thompson went to the Peterborough Police to assume leadership there.

The *Border Cities Star* lamented the failure of the Commission in not disclosing its findings, but stressed, "the main thing, of course, is that Mr. Thompson is no longer connected with the Windsor Police Department." The newspaper believed that as a result of Thompson's departure, along with the exposure given to so many gambling spots and blind pigs, "the underworld has been badly shaken."

That December, Curry, who in the previous municipal election had finished 15th in the polls, now led voting over all by some 1,500 votes.

7

Morality

Public morality has always been an issue, especially where it concerns police. Throughout the Border Cities during the Roaring Twenties, charges against officers and whole departments were almost a daily occurrence. As in Windsor, Ford City was the subject of investigation, too. In October 1924, a petition was brought to council that the police department had failed to curb the "general immorality" in the town. A special meeting of the Police, Fire, Water and Light Committee determined that the charges brought against police were unfounded, that there was "no tangible evidence of an unusual amount of crime in Ford City." The committee reported that the evidence given was "almost entirely of hearsay nature and totally unreliable." It was maintained that the police officers had been "diligent and prompt in the execution of their duties."

To some degree, this might have been true, but within the boundaries of the municipality, the effects of Prohibition were in evidence. Down the street from where municipal officials met was a house built only a few years earlier, and in some ways it set the tone for the times. This was a three-story building without floors – designed exclusively for the storage of liquor. Years later when its owners sold it, the new owners had to install two floors.

The first revolver used by the Ford City Police Department and Inspector's badge. Windsor Police Service Museum.

8
Walking the Beat at Ouellette & Sandwich
and How My Landlady Didn't Wake Me

Laxity within the Windsor Police was apparent throughout the period following the turn of the century and through the Roaring Twenties. The most common offence among police constables was an inability to be on time, and to be sober. Another problem was the frequency of constables drinking in saloons while on duty.

It seems walking the beat wasn't always the most stimulating task. Especially at Ouellette and Sandwich. There is one funny story about a Constable Watson in August 1916 reprimanded for gossiping at the corner for 10 minutes between 10:25 p.m. and 10:35 p.m., and for "standing in a slovenly position." The next month, a Constable Claude Renaud, later police chief of the Windsor Force, was docked one day's pay for "gossiping and inattention" while on duty at the corner of Ouellette and Sandwich. Another officer in January 1918 was given nine extra hours duty for being absent for 25 minutes from that corner. It didn't help, either, that his uniform wasn't properly clean. The reason for being absent from the corner from 8:45 a.m. to 9:20 a.m. was that he was "getting warm" and had stepped indoors along the way. Another officer, Constable McNally was criticized for removing a traffic sign from that same corner before the proper time.

Being on time was also a problem. Constable Clements in 1918 was

EACH YEAR THE DETROIT RIVER GIVES UP SOME OF THESE RELICS. WHERE THEY CAME FROM; WHO THREW THEM IN THE RIVER. WHAT THEY WERE USED FOR. WE MAY NEVER KNOW.

Windsor Police Service Museum.

disciplined after turning up for work 15 minutes late. He blamed his landlady for not waking him up on time. Another patrolman in 1922 was chastised because he was found napping in "the hallway of the Royal Bank building on Ouellette Avenue."

9

Fingers & The Inspector
The Story of The Bureau of Identification

He was called "The Inspector" by everyone, and when he retired from the Windsor Police Force in the summer of 1954 on his 65th birthday, he had been working on a number of things for which he had hoped he would have answers. While time may have run out for him "officially," he hoped to continue privately.

James Wilkinson was one of the best known experts in the science of criminology and identification in North America. He was the first to give evidence on the strength of fingerprint data in a Canadian criminal court. In this important test case, his testimony was accepted, and the accused convicted.

Wilkinson also proved to be the first in the world to make identification on fingerprint evidence through use of the telephone. In this case, he called a Detroit expert with more complete files, reading off the summary of data.

From left, Inspector James Wilkinson, Chief Claude Renaud, County Constable S.R. Kelly and Detective Stephens . Examining guns for clues. ws.

Wilkinson, too, is credited with inventing the system of applying graphite to a print with a camel hair brush, then lifting it from the surface with gummed transparent material. Before this, the print had to be photographed directly, and the results weren't always satisfactory.

It was by an obsessive and militant devotion to this science that Constable James H. Wilkinson developed the Identification Bureau of the Windsor Police, in fact, establishing the first such bureau in Canada, and one that soon became the envy of other departments on both sides of the border. Wilkinson had gone to Scotland after serving in the Canadian Medical Corps during the First World War, and took a six week course at Scotland Yard. It was there he got a taste for the science of fingerprint identification.

Till then, fingerprinting was still new. Before its development, criminals were identified by branding them, or tattooing them, even by amputating one of their limbs. Other methods developed which included photography and the Bertillon system, a technique based on the measurements of body parts.

Inspector James R. Wilkinson,
founder of the Identification
Bureau. ws.

It was in the 1880s that fingerprinting became a science. Sir Francis
Galton, a British anthropologist calculated that no two persons could
have exactly the same patterns in their fingerprints. Ten years later, two
police officers – Juan Vucetich of Argentina and Sir Edward R. Henry of
Great Britain developed a classification system for fingerprints. The
Henry system is what Wilkinson would have been familiar with when he
returned to Windsor. It was used widely in the U.S. Wilkinson was in
touch with Edward Foster of the Dominion Police (later renamed The
Royal Canadian Mounted Police) who advocated fingerprinting over
the Bertillon system. It was Foster's persistence that led to a repository
of fingerprints being created in Ottawa.

Prior to Wilkinson's interest in this science, he had worked for the
Canadian Pacific Railway Police in Windsor. So excited by what he had
learned at Scotland Yard, Wilkinson wrote to Chief Constable Elias
Wills to ask if he might hire him. The chief told him to return to
Windsor, because a job was waiting for him.

This was the first camera used by the Identification Branch to photograph crime scenes. Windsor Police Service Museum.

Wilkinson's skills in identification weren't tapped immediately. He started out directing traffic on Ouellette Avenue. When he got up enough nerve to broach the subject of an identification unit for the police, Wills agreed, advising the rookie to use time off to study it further in Detroit.

Chief Thompson's arrival on the force in 1921 was fortunate for Wilkinson. The young officer was put to work taking fingerprint impressions, photographs, and assembling files in the basement of what was then the City Hall. In time, the new unit was serving most police forces in southwestern Ontario. Wilkinson's hard work led a promotion to sergeant a year later, and in 1945 he was named superintendent.

It is said that during his time with the force, he worked seven days a week, and didn't take a vacation until 1946. He had gone 26 years without taking time away from the force.

Wilkinson is recognized as the pioneer of this branch of criminology. He was one of the first to form the amputation and tattoo files, which were helpful to detectives making identification. He was remembered for his minute studies of such things as laundry marks and handwriting. He was among the first in the country to study poroscopy, in which the shape and contour of the pores in the human skin are studied. Even today, experimentation continues with this. Wilkinson was dabbling in this in the 1940s and 50s. He was also studying papers on a German theory that the back of the eye of a corpse, for several hours following a death, retains an image of the last scene caught by the eye. Wilkinson was familiar with German studies that claimed it was possible to photograph this "last image." He believed this would be invaluable in solving

Fingerprinting equipment.
Windsor Police Service Museum.

Used by the Identification Branch.
Windsor Police Service Museum.

More than one million records were on file in the Windsor Police Identification and Records Bureau in 1945. ws.

murder cases. He attempted to photograph such an image from the eye of a corpse, but the equipment used was inadequate for the demands this experiment presented.

So famous was Wilkinson that it was not uncommon for J. Edgar Hoover of the FBI to visit him in Windsor. Wilkinson's family remembers Hoover as a regular guest at the house. So casual was it that often an extra plate was put out at dinner for him.

Wilkinson was born in Leeds, England. He joined the Yorkshire Constabulary in 1907, and remained with them for five years, walking a beat. He came to Canada in 1912 and worked for the CPR railway police in Toronto. During the war, he served with the Canadian Army. He died two years after his retirement from the Windsor Police Force.

It was apparent that many of his investigations – done mostly on behalf of the neighboring communities, including Walkerville, Ford City, Riverside, Essex, Leamington and even on occasion for the Ontario

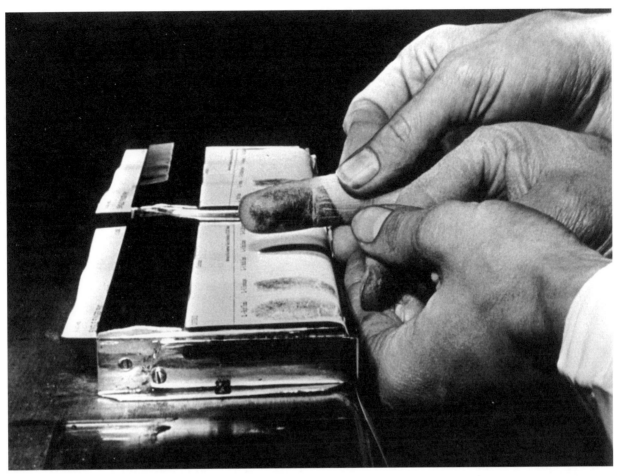

Without fingerprinting the Windsor Police Department would have a difficult time searching out records of criminals and the backgrounds of suspects with police records. ws.

Provincial Police and the CPR – produced astonishing results. He picked up one man's prints from a single piece of broken glass at the scene of a break-in in Walkerville. This print led police to make a criminal arrest, and to extradite the man to the U.S. when it was discovered he was still listed as a prisoner in the Arizona State Prison.

Wilkinson was involved in the arrest of another man after the chief of police in Knoxville, Tennessee sent a set of fingerprints of someone who was held for robbery in that city. Classification of that man's prints determined that he was living in Windsor. Further investigation uncovered that he was wanted for murder and for escaping from prison in Indianapolis. The man, who thought he had duped police all over Ontario, was surprised at the arrest. Stories commending the work of the Windsor Police appeared in newspapers in both Knoxville and Indianapolis.

Another story has it that Wilkinson's work led to the arrest of a man

Communications equipment in use in 1935. Windsor Police Service Museum.

named Alvin Lee whom the Ontario Provincial Police were looking for in connection with armed robberies. This man had never been arrested in Windsor. The acquisition of a set of prints from the Detroit Police, however, helped to identify him. It wasn't without work, or ingenuity. A search through more than 12,000 prints determined that a man, calling himself Harry Burke, and being held in custody for trespassing upon the property of the Michigan Central, was indeed Alvin Lee. He believed he couldn't be identified, because since he was last fingerprinted, three of fingers had been amputated from his left hand. Wilkinson proved him wrong.

In another case, Wilkinson assisted the RCMP solve a mail theft case in LaSalle. Extensive fingerprinting at the post office helped police track down a young man in a nearby boathouse. Wilkinson was there to fingerprint the man while the thief was still asleep in bed. Matching those prints with those from the scene of the crime resulted in his conviction.

In the 1923 annual report, Chief Constable Thompson noted that other chief constables told him the Windsor Identification Bureau was far ahead of the rest of the country. He maintained that the Chief Constables' Association of Canada, meeting in Windsor, was "greatly

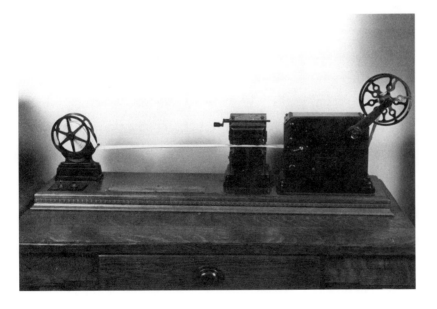

The "Call Box" system used by the Windsor Police from 1921 to 1974. Above is the call box switchboard; and below, the "pen register" that operated a tape that would signal the call box and alert the constable on the beat to call headquarters. Windsor Police Service Museum.

astonished" by the facilities organized by Wilkinson. He also pointed out that John Shea, the St. Louis, Mo., superintendent of the Bureau of Identification – the first to establish the finger printing system in the U.S. in 1901 – was impressed by Windsor's introduction of the "Cross Index System of Circulars and Men Wanted." Windsor pioneered the way in both Canada and the U.S. with this system, again entirely on the initiative of Wilkinson. Shea promised to copy the system on his return to St. Louis.

Political cartoon from 1920s. ws

10
Prohibition
Those Wild and Wooly Days

During the wild and wooly days of the Roaring Twenties, the Border Cities and the Border police forces teetered on the edge of scandal and respectability. There were few heroes on the side of the law – mostly because the romance of the era fell to those breaking the rules. They were the ones becoming millionaires. When Prohibition came into being in January 1920 in the U.S., the feeling was that a New Age had dawned, that clean living North Americans would no longer be harassed by Demon Rum. Nonetheless, in Canada, many unlikely individuals saw the opportunity to profit from the new laws.

What the prohibitionists failed to understand was just how entrenched liquor was in society, that it wasn't merely just a means for intoxication, but a way of life. Saloons in the U.S. outnumbered the churches and hospitals and schools. They were places to keep warm, to have lunch, to unwind, to play darts, to converse and to spend a day in quiet or celebration. The prohibitionists saw it as the root of all evil, the road to Hell. And when Prohibition came it effect, it set the stage for the colorful and high-flying Roaring Twenties.

In this area, it became clear that the border would become the conduit for liquor going into the U.S. Indeed four fifths of all the booze flowing from Canada to the U.S. went through Windsor, as regular as the Windsor-Detroit Ferry, in fact, often on the ferry boat itself.

Charles Johnson, formerly of Ford City Police. ws

Constable at the Export Docks

Before Prohibition, Charles Johnson worked for the Ford City Police Department as a motorcycle driver. He joined the Windsor force in 1935 at the time of amalgamation, and was appointed a sergeant. In 1963, he retired, having spent 44 years in police work on the border. In all, he had

Police in Sandwich after raid in 1923. Windsor Police Service Museum.

worked just about every detail – from the bomb squad and bootlegging to detective and homicide.

Johnson found the rumrunning days the most demanding. The export docks were strung out along the riverfront then like "some huge bootlegging dream," he said. Johnson patrolled them, acquainting himself with rumrunners, exporters, and the seamier side, including Al Capone. The Chicago gangster had visited Windsor a number of times to make deals down at the Ford City Export dock. "He was there dickering with the exporters about liquor. He came down to see Harris and Caplan who ran the dock. I suppose he wanted to know who was the best here to haul his liquor. Capone would take a thousand cases a day out of the docks here."

In those days, Johnson said, police conducted raids almost daily. They would smash down doors, axe crates of whiskey, dump liquor into the river, arrest bootleggers, shut down blind pigs, and at times, even battle the rumrunners in the streets or on the waterfront.

Johnson described the rumrunners as clever and brash. Only a few were businessmen. Most were small-time operators who picked up

Cecil Smith. ws

boats and hauled the whiskey in the dead of night. Many became so attuned to running contraband whiskey across the border that they had figured out all the angles. That meant bribing, clever ways of concealing booze, designing faster cars and more efficient engines for speedboats, rigging up signals and lights, sending out decoy boats and "just plain outwitting the customs and police." Many hauled whiskey in sprawling Chandlers or Studebakers with the back seats removed to make room for crates from Hiram Walker and Sons.

One man who gave him trouble was the swaggering, brash, tough Cecil Smith whom Johnson considered unlucky. "He was always getting caught." Bootlegging was second nature to Smith. It was an integral part of his life, and the Windsor Police could easily claim that whenever his hulking figure was stopped for a routine search – even as late as the 1950s – invariably a few mickeys were buried within the deep pockets of his overcoat.

But if a jail sentence frightened Cecil Smith, it certainly never deterred him in the business of booze. Johnson said, "In the beginning he was just a small guy . . . but then he made millions. Oh, he was steal-

Models demonstrate the extraordinary measures taken to get illegal alcohol across the border. ws

The prisoner that was travelling in this car with Constable Morel took his own life en route to the police station. He was a suspect in several robberies and in the shooting of an Ottawa Street merchant . The year was 1932. ws.

ing whiskey from other guys, but so were they . . . I remember him as a quiet, easygoing guy . . . never cantankerous, but when he wanted to be in a fighting mood, watch out."

True enough. One night during Prohibition, Smith attempted to steal a boxcar of booze, but was caught by a Windsor constable, William Allen. Smith had seven trucks and five touring cars ready to load up 750 cases. Allen tried to stop them, so Smith offered the officer $2,000. When Allen refused the bribe, Smith beat him up and handcuffed him to the boxcar, and left with the shipment.

In court later, Smith remarked, "The next time I offer Allen $2,000, he will prefer it to being beaten up."

In another case, Johnson once seized 250 cases of whiskey on the ice between the mainland and Peche Island. A truck had carried the cases

J. O. L. Spracklin, "The Fighting Parson" (left), with his "personal bodyguard", Sgt. Duncan Macnab of the Windsor Police. ws.

out near the open water where a boat was to pick up the shipment. Johnson and fellow officers circled around the ice and confiscated the whiskey before the boat arrived.

"The rumrunners had plenty of ideas on how to avoid detection. Some of them tried to drive loads of whiskey across Lake St. Clair on the ice. They would carry heavy planks and when they came to a piece of open water they made a bridge."

Johnson was also involved in the investigation of the case of Michael Zone whose body was found floating in shallow water near the Canadian shore. Zone had cashed in $3,000 in bonds the day before to make a trip to his home in Europe.

"Marks on the body," said Johnson, "showed he had been murdered and thrown into the river. The money was missing."

Zone's murder, as many others, went unsolved.

The Fighting Parson

The gun-toting Methodist minister Rev. J. O. L. Spracklin's shooting of Beverley "Babe" Trumble epitomized the dramatic confrontation that

existed during Prohibition between the temperance forces and the
whiskey dealers. It is his story – the shooting at the Chappell House in
Sandwich Street – that captured the attention of both sides of the
border. That incident occurred in the early morning hours of Nov. 6,
1920. Spracklin turned himself into the Windsor Police – not the
Sandwich force, for he believed he'd get a fairer hearing.

The story of this confrontation itself arises out of a boyhood rivalry
between Spracklin and Trumble. When Prohibition came into effect,
Trumble was the owner of a roadhouse. Spracklin was the pastor of
Sandwich Methodist, just down the street. The flashy Trumble had little
difficulty making friends, and drawing in crowds to his Chappell House.
Right from the beginning of Prohibition, he began to reap its benefits
from serving contraband liquor, and providing gambling and game-
cock fights. Spracklin, an individualist who kept to himself, had few
friends, and languished on low pay from the church. Worse was the
impotence he felt at not being able to wield moral influence over the
situation that plagued the Border Cities. He yearned for an end to the

Above photograph shows federal agents throwing contraband whiskey into the Detroit River, while bottom photograph shows the arrangements made by rumrunners to take whiskey across the river. ws

abuses of Prohibition. The target of his demands centred upon Trumble whose roadhouse boomed with music at all hours of the night. As Spracklin plotted his strategy to face Trumble, he couldn't foretell how much he would become a metaphor for his times.

It was in June 1920 that Spracklin finally confronted the issue, towering above a cowering Sandwich Town Council, and demanding an investigation into the widespread sale of liquor in the municipality. He told council that the town had become "a dumping ground for the lowest element; an element which we might well be rid of and which comes to us from all parts of the United States to obtain what they are looking for – strong drink."

He reported that "at any time of the night, you can hear men passing your street door using the most obscene language; drunken, rolling, spewing, fighting men in all stages of intoxication. . . "

The target of his attack, too, was Alois Master, chief Constable for Sandwich. Spracklin claimed that one night he counted 30 drunken men and women leaving the Chappell House while Master sat on the front steps "twirling his thumbs." Spracklin claimed one girl in a drunken stupor actually sat for a moment on Master's lap before he told her to get moving.

His criticism was met with opposition throughout the town, especially from Trumble and Master. But Spracklin wouldn't back down. Less than a week later, buoyed up by rumors that William E. Raney, the provincial attorney general, was ready to step in to correct the situation, the pastor warned he would lay charges against the Sandwich police chief under the Ontario Temperance Act.

Although Sandwich Council tried to deflect Spracklin's charges, Raney appointed the Methodist minister as a free-lance liquor licence inspector. He was also given use of a large touring car, a launch for the Detroit River, and the right to hire 24 more inspectors. The men Spracklin hired – the famous Halam brothers – were thugs. In essence, he had more power than most police forces in the region.

Spracklin's appointment infuriated Inspector M. N. Mousseau, who claimed they worked at odds with one another. Spracklin maintained he was doing the work that should have been done all along.

Unlike other inspectors, Spracklin used firearms. As a matter of fact, he wore guns on his hips, even during services at the church. He trusted no one, often sending thugs to search through the automobiles and carriages of his parishioners while they worshipped in the sanctuary. "The Fighting Parson," as he came to be called, also began using blank search warrants. Soon he came under criticism for taking the matter of Demon Rum too far. One police commission committee member asked, "Why not have martial law and be done with it?" Spracklin's

Rumrunners bought old jalopies, loaded them with crates of whiskey, and drove them across the ice to waiting customers. ws

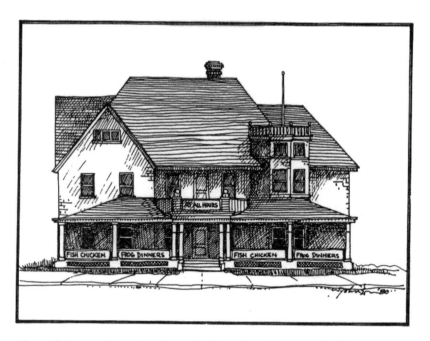

Chappell House where shooting took place. Gervais personal collection.

quick retort was: "Well, you'll have that unless conditions are soon cleared up."

His war on rumrunners came to a halting end, however, in November of 1920 when he stole into the Chappell House and shot and killed Trumble. "It was his life or mine," a tired Spracklin confessed to Windsor police when he turned himself in. He claimed Trumble had pulled a gun on him. The case didn't go to trial immediately. In fact, the pastor was only charged after mounting public criticism. Some 2,000 signatures supported the demand for a trial. Raney relented and announced that Spracklin would be charged with manslaughter.

In the end, the Fighting Parson was found to be innocent, but the trial was an international story, drawing reporters from all parts of the U.S. as well as Europe. Police stationed outside the courtroom barred hundreds of individuals who had attempted to carry weapons into the trial. It was certain that Spracklin's life was in danger.

When the jury finally deliberated, it returned its verdict in 59 minutes, saying Spracklin would be set free. The gun-toting pastor was back in court a month later, and fined $500 for trespassing on the yacht of Oscar Fleming, a Windsor lawyer, and son of Windsor's first mayor.

Eventually, Spracklin left Windsor, taking up work in Michigan. He died in Greenbush, Michigan May 28, 1960. He was 73.

PART THREE

Amalgamation, Cleanup, the Beginning of Stability
1935 – 1968

Mortimer Wigle was Chief
Constable of the police force at the
time of amalgamation.

Chief Maisonville of East Windsor
Police

1
The New Border Police

At the time of amalgamation of Windsor, Sandwich, Walkerville and
East Windsor, the feeling was that a unified force would be, as the *Star*
suggested, "an effective arm against crime."

In 1935, following the choppy, chaotic years of the Roaring Twenties
when people openly defied the law, things seemed quieter, less exacting.
Newspapers at the time described crime as "more casual." Nonetheless
with the melding of four communities stretched out along the Detroit
River, coupled with the growth of organized crime across the water, and
the city in the grip of the Great Depression, it became apparent that it
would be necessary to marshal an effective deterrent to crime.

To effect this transformation, the Windsor Police hired Chief James
P. Smith of the Walkerville Police. Although Mortimer Wigle had been
its first choice – and the desire of the other departments merging with
Windsor's – he declined. When Smith was asked how the transition
would be handled, he told reporters at the *Star* that "Rome was not built
in a day, nor will the new city of Windsor . . ." He also pointed out that
whatever plans he might have, he would first present them to the police
commission. Indeed, he pointed out, "It might be several months before
the police department is working on a permanent basis."

His first move was to divide the city into "precincts," along the lines
of the old departments. Albert "Toppy" Maisonville, chief of East
Windsor, and J. D. Proctor, chief of Sandwich, were both named police
inspectors under the new force. Smith expressed hope at the time of his
appointment that the precincts would be linked by a radio system. For
the time being, the new chief said, telephone lines would have to suffice.

The development of law enforcement in Sandwich, East Windsor
and Walkerville had followed the pattern in Windsor. In the early days,
these forces were "one man" operations, with the chief constables depu-
tizing appropriate individuals. East Windsor, formerly Ford City, was
the newest. Ed Moran was the chief of Ford City in those early days.
Albert, or "Toppy," Maisonville succeeded him and held that position
till 1935 when the force merged with the Windsor force at amalgamation. Maisonville was made an inspector with the Windsor Police. He
was 52. He had been on the Ford City Force since 1914. By 1935, as its
Chief, the force had grown to be 17 men strong.

Walkerville's force arose from Hiram Walker's own company-
managed plant protection officers, headed by A. B. Griffith. This was
when the area was called Walker's Town. These officers, employed by
Walker, maintained law and order not only in the plant, but in the
village. The fire department and for that matter even other officials from

The East Windsor Police
Department. Windsor Police
Service Museum.

the village were employed by Walker. When Walkerville was incorporated as a town in 1890, Griffith became police chief. Smith, who had started with the force in 1900, took over its administration in 1921.

From the time of incorporation in 1858 until 1894, Sandwich was policed primarily by county officers. In fact, it was so haphazard that often, the turnkey at the county jail was assigned to handle criminal matters. If it turned out to be something serious, or dangerous, a county officer would be called in.

One of the earliest constables in Sandwich was Alois Master who for 30 years was a county constable. Later he became High County Constable for Essex County. Master, born in Germany in 1844, settled in Sandwich in 1857. For several years, he served as bailiff for the Essex County First Division Court. In 1894, he was named chief of Sandwich. He was joined by Gordon Pillon just after the turn of the century, bringing the force to a total of two men.

While Master was police chief, his duties also included being "dog catcher" for the municipality. He was given some jurisdiction, too, over the fire department, and even acted as inspector of health. Eventually, Pillon succeeded him as Chief, followed by Bob Synder. J. D. Proctor, a veteran of the RCMP was named chief of the nine-man force.

Smith's new force in 1935 boasted a staff of 112 men, 77 of whom were patrolmen. At the time of amalgamation, the Windsor force had 57 patrolmen with 23 others who were either officers or who performed special duties.

The old Walkerville jail, torn down in 1954 to make way for an enlarged shipping yard for Hiram Walker and Sons. It was built at the turn of the century. ws.

2
The Man Who Did Not Want To Be Chief

That fateful morning in 1935 when James Paton Smith got up to shave and get ready to go downtown to the police station, he had great plans for the new Windsor Police Force. And he had spoken of them to his wife, and to his friends. One ponders how things might have turned out had his sterling record carried over to the new force. As chief for only a few days, he had been battling an illness that actually required him to take a leave. He decided to return to the job earlier than what his doctors might have wished. That morning while shaving in the bathroom, he died of a heart attack.

Smith had not wanted the job of organizing the amalgamated police force that folded Walkerville, Ford, Sandwich and Windsor into one. He was 60, and had been chief of the Walkerville Police Force for 14 years. He felt that, Mortimer Wigle, who had been police chief in Windsor before amalgamation, should continue. Wigle told the Finance Commission in May 1935 that he didn't want the job. Neither did Smith. "I don't want the position if Mort Wigle thinks he can continue," said Smith to the Commissioners. He added sincerely, "I would be willing to serve under Mort in any capacity."

Smith, the crisp-looking, straight-standing policeman with a handlebar mustache, was everyone's choice. He had 35 years of police experience, both as a Provincial Police officer, and later as a constable in Walkerville. The *Border Cities Star* said the task of reshaping the new force was "heavier than the ordinary citizen could believe, but he was making definite progress toward an ideal and had succeeded in winning the confidence and respect of the men under his command."

Smith had proven himself as a tenacious police constable over the years. The son of a baker, born near Barrie, Ont., he moved with his family to Walkerville where he worked in his father's shop and drove a delivery wagon. Smith started with the Walkerville Police April 1, 1900, and worked there patrolling a beat with A. Mapes for three years. He then became a county constable, and held that job for six years after which he received his appointment as an Ontario Provincial Police constable.

It was during that time he joined up with Nash in a fearless intervention that saved the Windsor Armouries from being bombed during the First World War. Three men – Albert Lefler, Charles Respa and Albert Kaltschmidt – dynamited the Peabody Building, and had planned to do the same at the Armouries. After the blast shook the first building, both Smith and Nash were dispatched to the site. Lefler was arrested immediately after the blast, and Respa escaped. A few weeks later, he was taken into custody in Detroit. The third member – Kaltschmidt – was arrested in Detroit, too, and sentenced for an act against a friendly country.

It was Respa's arrest, however, that demonstrated the wily demeanor of Smith and Nash. He had been watched for several weeks by informers. The two policemen were waiting for just the right moment when Respa might cross the border back into Canada. When it was learned he was going to a picnic on Bob-Lo Island, the two policemen headed for Amherstburg, crossed over to the island, and arrested him on Canadian soil as he stepped off the boat. Respa was sentenced to life imprisonment, and was freed after the armistice.

During the First World War, Smith had been refused entry into the army by Toronto authorities when he tried to enlist – ironic, since he had served as a regimental sergeant-major with the old 21st Fusiliers. He had joined that unit in 1892 and continued with the militia for 22 years. In

Chief James P. Smith of the Walkerville Police Department. ws.

Walkerville Police in front of the Walkerville Jail. Chief Smith is the third person from the left. ws.

1911, Smith was awarded the Coronation medal, and the following year received the Canadian Militia's long service medal.

During the war, it was felt that Smith's contribution might be greater at rounding up spies and conspirators, as proven with the Peabody bombing.

Bill Butcher, one of the owners of Butcher Engineering, and whose family lived in Walkerville, recalled Smith. He was a boy when the police chief approached him and his brother, Les, to help train his police dogs.

"He used to keep these bloodhounds at the corner of Lincoln and Wyandotte, and he was training them. He'd let the dogs smell us up and down, and then he'd give us a nickel each to go and hide in the bush – in what is now South Walkerville. And we'd go and hide there, and he'd let the dogs try and find us."

When Smith returned to the Walkerville force in 1921 as Chief, he was responsible for building up the department. His efforts won both it and him recognition across the country, for this force came to be regarded as the most efficient force in the country – especially for its small size, and considering the enormity of the task when the area was in the throes of Prohibition. In spite of the era – and the utter disregard of the law during the Roaring Twenties – Smith's force kept matters in check. Walkerville proved to have less serious crime within its boundaries than any similar municipality in Canada. The year before he became the first chief after amalgamation, Walkerville had no more than 75 cases in its police court. Half that number represented drunk and traffic charges. And for a month and a half, there was not a single case listed in the court. This was believed to be a record for any municipality of the town's status.

Recognition came to Smith in 1931 when he was appointed president of the Chief Constables Association of Canada. The Canadian Police Bulletin that year singled out Smith as an outstanding law enforcer. The Bulletin stated that "the absence of serious juvenile crime should be credited in part at least to the activities of Chief Smith himself who is a real friend of the boys and ever alert to look after their interests and protect them from evil influences."

But while it would seem that Smith met with little opposition in Walkerville, the early days were tough ones. As the *Border Cities Star* reported:

He came to grips frequently with desperate characters and often his fine physique stood him in good stead. He had experiences with murderers, armed horse thieves, burglars, hold-up men and rum smugglers and seldom came off second best in his encounters. While on occasion he was obliged to use force in making his capture he found that a kindly reasonableness was the most efficient weapon at his command.

Parking regulation signs
ca. 1934. Windsor Police
Service.

The Ford Motor Company of Canada strike, 1945. ws.

It had been thought that with joining the Windsor force, Smith might have brought a discipline that was sadly needed. This would have to wait.

3
Housekeeping after Amalgamation

In 1936, a year after amalgamation, Chief Claude Renaud, who succeeded Smith, ordered his 100-man department to canvass every store and house in the city to ensure that the municipality's bylaws were being enforced properly. He reported that inspectors checked to make sure that all dog, milk, garage and other necessary licences were taken out. The old "bread bylaw" was still in effect then, and Renaud revealed that a number of cases of shortweight bread were investigated. Coal shipments to homes were also weighed.

In those first years after amalgamation Renaud called for stricter control over traffic in the city. In 1939, he complained that a favorable exchange rate on the American dollar had attracted more visitors from Michigan – to the extent that the business area of Windsor had become congested. He also promised a clamp down on motorists who had been using bus stops for parking. It was Renaud's suggestion that year to have bus stop signs erected. Till then, the S. W. & A Bus Company provided painted markers on the curbs.

Confrontation between police and striking workers at Ford of Canada, 1945. ws.

4
The Ford Strike

One wonders how serious a problem the 1945 Ford Strike was to Windsor Police. Chief Constable Claude Renaud's annual report failed

Chief of Police, Claude Renaud. ws.

to cite it as an occurrence. Instead he noted three murders. He also devoted discussion to the proposed purchase of new police cruisers. The strike is never mentioned. Yet, there is no question it posed a problem to the police, and to the city.

From September through till November, the subject of the strike consumed the police commission's time. It was daily reading, too, in the *Star*.

When the Second World War ended in August 1945 with the defeat of Japan, it was clear that employees of the Ford Motor Company in old Ford City were ready to strike. The United Auto Workers (UAW) in Windsor had received certification to form a union in November 1941. A certification ballot, supervised by the federal Department of Labor, resulted in a vote of 6,833 in favor of a union, with 4,455 registering their opposition. On Dec. 1, 1944, the UAW Local 200 received its charter.

After 18 months of futile talks, the union knew that it wasn't going to get the company to budge. The unresolved issues centred around seniority rights, medical provisions, lay-off procedures and paid vacations. On September 12, 1945, workers decided they had had enough, and began a strike that would last 99 days and go down in the history books as that moment when Canadian labor won the guarantee of union security.

Public support for the strike was high throughout the city. And naturally, the consummately-political Mayor Art Reaume was there to throw vigorous support behind the workers. He vowed that no "imported police force" would be used to break the strike. The police, however, were under pressure to do something to open up the strike lines, so that managers could get into the plant. On that first day, Ford Canada president Wallace R. Campbell, in attempting to cross the picket lines, was confronted by an army of angry strikers who stood their ground with placards and threats.

The *Star* reported Local 200's president Roy England climbing aboard a truck, pledging that Campbell would be fought to "the bitter end." He vowed, "This city will not return to the breadlines and soup kitchens of the pre-war years."

Ford registered its complaints immediately. The day after the strike began, the police commission was faced with the dilemma involving its police in the dispute. While it was agreed that the police should not countenance any breach of the law, the Commission stated that Ford was permitted under law to send its officials into the plant.

Peace reigned over the picket lines for more than a month, but the company was still frustrated by picketers who inhibited its supervisors from getting into the building. Ford mounted still more pressure upon the Commission for help.

After six weeks, the real confrontation occurred. The company reported that it wished to get its 110 plant protection officers past the strikers. It argued that the protection of its estimated $6 million "power house" was vital, and warned that if regular maintenance wasn't done, then extreme temperatures could result in damage to the machinery itself, and possibly in an explosion and fire. Ford backed its claim up with an insurance report. The union wouldn't acquiesce.

The Commission deliberated over the issue for a few days, then on Nov. 2 resolved that Renaud should take necessary steps to get Ford's 101-member protective force past the strikers. More importantly, the Commission resolved, if the Windsor Police needed "additional police," then it should be assured "necessary assistance." Reaume protested and abstained from voting.

With that, Ottawa sent in the RCMP, who were joined by the Ontario Provincial Police. This small army was unable to carry out its mandate of separating the strikers. On Nov. 5, thousands of honking cars formed

Chief Claude Renaud. ws

a blockade, jamming some 20 blocks surrounding the plant, making the way impenetrable. With that, the police were in full retreat. So was the police commission. As the blockade persisted, aid from across North America poured in for the strikers who had been living on a meagre strike pay of $6 a week.

In time, the two sides realized that neither was going to relent, and so they agreed to binding arbitration. Justice Ivan Rand was summoned to sort out the contentious issues. Rand condemned the union for its "lawlessness," and Ford for its "intransigence." When he handed down his decision, he rejected the notion of a "union shop," where all personnel would be required to join. At the same time, he agreed that "it (was) entirely equitable that all employees should be required to shoulder their portion of the burden" of the costs incurred by a union in negotiating a contract for all employees.

The solution Rand brought was called "The Rand Formula," the historic step made in guaranteeing union security.

5
Gotch Ya!

In January 1950, Windsor Police got an edge over speeders when its police cars were outfitted with "special speedometers," or a new device operated in much the same way as a stop watch. The needle revolved in the same manner as a conventional meter but could be stopped at any point by pushing a button. When a speeder was caught and claimed he was not going over the limit, the officer would lead him back to the cruiser, point to the speed at which the needle stopped, and give him a ticket.

This new device replaced one where the police had to allow about 10 mph over the limit because of possible discrepancies in the regular type of meter. The new equipment, according to police, was made "like precision watches, and the works have jewels similar to those of timepieces."

6
Dodging Snowballs & Dodging Trouble
The Fifties Scandal, and the Story of Chief Claude Renaud

When Crime Was King

The day Claude Renaud started with the Windsor Police on the first day of March 1915, he found himself pelted with snowballs from the tough

"Church Street" gang. When he retired in 1950, he had fled a much harsher pelting – that of public criticism in a scandal that rocked the city and its police force. Although Chief Renaud had been exonerated of any wrongdoing by the Windsor Police Commission which stated that he had "carried out his duties honestly and to the best of (his) ability," it was evident that his leadership had failed to quash the corruption and laxity that permeated his department.

Chief Renaud's controversial retirement followed a series of events which began with a judgment given by Magistrate J. A. Hanrahan on March 8, 1950. The judge sentenced bootlegger Joe Assef to six months in jail. He castigated the police for having permitted this man to operate freely and build up a business which made 5,400 deliveries of liquor in 60 days.

That judgment caused Attorney General Dana H. Porter the next day to launch an investigation into the bootlegger's activities. In the mean-

The first investigation of the Windsor Police Department by the Police Commission in September 1950 prior to the Claude Renaud scandal. From left, Colonel Harris, Chief Renaud, Mayor Reaume, and Judge Cochrane. ws

Magistrate Angus MacMillan. ws

Mayor Art Reaume. ws

time, the Windsor Police Commission – comprising of Mayor Arthur J. Reaume, Magistrate Angus. W. MacMillan and Judge A. J. Gordon – was summoned to Toronto and ordered to conduct a thorough investigation of charges of laxity in law enforcement.

Four days later, A. Douglas Bell, K.C., Chatham Crown Attorney was appointed by the police commission as counsel for the investigation into "allegations of corruption."

The Commission's probe began March 16. Witness after witness paraded by testifying there was absolutely no corruption among the police. But Porter wasn't satisfied. Neither was Premier Leslie Frost who warned if the Commission didn't take action, he would.

When the Commission's probe was finished, Bell stated that Magistrate Hanrahan's statements had been "exaggerated" and "unjust."

The following month, Mayor Reaume and Magistrate MacMillan issued their own report calling for a provincial police inspector to take "temporary control" of the police department. Instead, Premier Frost and the Attorney General dispatched two inspectors to survey law enforcement procedures here, and to check out Detroit-Windsor underworld connections.

This provincial investigation was carried out during the summer of 1950. In September when their report was released, E. C. Awrey was removed as Crown Attorney in Windsor, and Magistrate MacMillan and Judge Gordon both resigned from the police commission.

The report stated there was "a decided lack of confidence by citizens of the existing law enforcement agencies in Windsor." It also contended that "most of the troubles" could be "laid at the doorstep of the morality detail." The investigating team discovered "wholesale betting and gambling that could not have been carried on without the knowledge of all members of the police department."

The probe also noted close connections between Detroit and Windsor gamblers and criminals. Investigators stated: "It is a matter of grave concern and this set-up would probably never have existed if the Windsor Police had taken vigorous action on the bookies some five years ago. The handbook operator makes corruption a science."

In an article, "When Crime Was King," Robert Pearson, former editor and publisher at the *Windsor Star,* and who had been a reporter during the 1950s, said that in spite of what was being voiced then by city officials – indeed the police department itself – one could walk down Ottawa Street, Drouillard Road, Pitt Street, even Ouellette and hear "the drone of the 'callers' on the race wire running down the results all over the continent... The bookies joints were usually only casually screened-in pool halls, shoe shine parlors, tobacco shops and in some cases legitimate retail establishments."

Pearson wrote, "You could walk in off the street and put down a bet with only one question asked, 'How much?'"

The race wire headquarters were situated in the old Murray Building at the northeast corner of Pitt and Ferry Streets. It was run by former employees of the telephone company. These technicians would pay a small fee to use someone's phone in the suburbs, and cleverly reroute a phone number, allowing it to ring in a bookie joint downtown.

In addition, the blind pig business was big. A carryover of laws from Prohibition still made it difficult to get access to drinks, especially after hours. The blind pigs catered to the carriage trade, and, by word of mouth or through taxi drivers, one could find out about places such as Fitz, Elmer's, and Dirty Kate's.

According to Pearson the practice among the police was to drag in "a straw man" into court, and make sure he was fined, but the blind pig or the bookie joints would stay open. It appeared as if the police were doing their job, when in fact, they were assisting the business.

The *Star* took it upon itself to wage its own campaign against the blatant disregard for justice. Pearson confided that Judge Hanrahan was the paper's modern day "deep throat," forever providing reporters and editors with leads.

Others in the city were concerned, too. One such man was jeweler and former Mayor Bert Weeks, only 29 when he arrived in Windsor. He was surprised by its dark side, and remarked that "people were disappearing; (and) people were being beaten up; there was a lot of violence."

He concluded organized crime couldn't flourish unless there was police complicity, and as a member of the Citizens Action Committee, he began to lobby for an investigation. In an interview with radio personality Paul Vasey in 1972, he revealed how he had gone to Detroit one night on a lead from a "hood" who offered him information about the involvement of high-placed officials in the city. When he told other committee members he was planning to rendezvous with this man across the river, they offered him a revolver. He dismissed their concerns. Nonetheless, he carried a jeweler's screwdriver.

"I thought if anyone stops me, I could say I was just going out to fix a clock."

The night was spent in fear, and in drinking beer with a gang of thugs who confided in him a list of the cops on the take. Weeks claimed it was this meeting – and what he passed on to the RCMP – that led to the revelations that shook City Hall.

Detroit's Police Commissioner Harry S. Troy seemed more interested in justice than those on this side. His warnings to Windsor, however, fell on deaf ears. He accused the Windsor Police of allowing

Graduates of a police training
course, 1949. ws

bookies to operate with impunity. It wasn't until the inquiry had
stormed into the affairs of the department that police began raids of
bookie joints in December 1950.

In the end, both Renaud and Deputy-Chief W. H. Neale were coerced
into retirement. Public opinion has always been that the two were
"fired" from their jobs, so the police department could be overhauled.
Judge Archibald Cochrane, chairman of the Windsor Police
Commission, stated at the end of the probe that the investigation had
confined itself "towards discovery of any weaknesses which may exist
within the Department and to determine what re-organization is necessary to obtain a strong and efficient police Force."

Cochrane said the conclusion that was reached was that "the interests of the Force" would be served best by the retirement of the chief and deputy-chief. And with that, the police commission asked Renaud and Neale to retire.

Staff Inspector Edwin V. McNeill of the Ontario Provincial Police took over the Windsor force until Carl W. Farrow was appointed in January 1951. A provincial police officer with experience from the rumrunning days, Farrow was dispatched here "to clean up the border," and that he did. Pearson said that when this move was made, the Windsor Police finally were on the road "to an efficiency and professionalism it had never known. This spirit has been maintained . . .'"

7

The Chief
Claude Renaud
1935 – 1950

It is one of those ironies that when Claude Renaud joined the Windsor Police in 1915, it wasn't really by choice. His sudden departure in 1950 may not have been by choice either. At the start of the First World War, the Windsor-born Renaud, who grew up on Erie Street the son of a blacksmith, was working as a buffer and polisher at Ford's. He left that to try police work, but decided that working seven days a week was too much, and that he would return to the factory as soon as a job came open.

As he told the *Star* on the 25th anniversary with the Windsor Police in 1940, "It just kind of got in my blood and so I decided to stick."

In those years with the department, when he was photographed in a double-breasted suit, and oozing with confidence, Renaud still was remembered as a tough-minded, poised, capable but laconic cop. There were only 20 men on the force when he started. Norman Hull, former editor at the *Windsor Star* wrote that Renaud had been "an officer of unusual merit" and found himself rising quickly in the ranks. He walked the beat downtown for two years before being promoted to the motorcycle squad.

A story from that period that Renaud used to tell is how once on his Harley Davidson motorcycle he chased a speeder along Sandwich Street, and in the process lost his revolver.

"I struck a hole in the street and fell off my bike. I got on again and caught the fellow. When I got back to the police station, I found that I had lost my gun."

About a year later when making another arrest, he found it in the pocket of another criminal. The revolver itself had special significance to Renaud. It was issued to him when he started with the Windsor Police. It was one of the first issues made to police. Renaud's handgun was No. 13. The manufacturer had been advised not to make a No. 13, but went ahead anyway. When it arrived at the department, there was so much superstition about accepting a No. 13 revolver, that no one would claim it. Renaud did, and kept the weapon all his life.

Two years after working on the motorcycle squad, Renaud was made a detective. His most interesting case was one involving Tony Miglio of Detroit in 1923. Miglio had come to Windsor, assaulted a man and returned to Detroit. Windsor Police didn't hear about the incident until the next day when the victim died at the hospital. Renaud, then a detective, was assigned to the case, and by the afternoon had tracked down Miglio in Detroit with a detective with the Detroit Police Force. Miglio was returned to Canada and arrested for murder. The charge was later reduced to manslaughter, but Miglio was sentenced to life imprisonment, and died in prison.

That was the kind of sleuth Renaud proved to be, and thus he came to the notice of the Michigan Central Railway which was looking for such a person to head their force in St. Thomas, Ont. Renaud left Windsor to join the railroad force, but two years later, was back. The five-foot-ten constable, who had learned his police work on the fly, was back in the city, not as a detective, but as an inspector, a position he held for five years until Chief Smith died. The police commission decided upon Renaud as a replacement – at the time, considered to be unusual considering that he had risen from constable to chief constable without ever being a sergeant on the force. When pressed to explain that, Renaud remarked to a *Star* reporter that it was "just lots of luck."

In the Windsor Police Commission minutes of Dec. 16, 1935, Mayor G. H. Bennett noted that 55-year-old Detective-Sergeant Duncan Macnab had an "enviable record" and that he should be made Chief. Magistrate D. M. Brodie on the other hand argued that the new chief should be "a man of a disposition different to that of Macnab's, and the Board could not afford to take any chances."

Brodie stated that during the past eight years he had observed Detective Inspector Renaud, and felt he had shown "great zeal." The magistrate also commended Renaud for "a splendid record." The police commission chairman Judge Coughlin agreed with the mayor, but believed Renaud was "the better man." With that, Renaud was declared the new police chief.

Two years later as chief, Renaud's investigation and arrest of a suspect resulted in the roundup of 13 car thieves.

His son, Ray Renaud, retired after 32 years with the Windsor Fire

Department, said his father was an amiable man who didn't hesitate to explain the full impact of the corruption scandal to his children during those stormy 50s .

"His biggest fault was that he was too soft, too easy with his own people. . . He was genuinely known as a great guy, but he didn't step on his own people."

While Renaud may have been "soft" on his department – perhaps too laid-back – he rarely backed down from trouble. Ray Renaud recounted once how his father – then police chief – hopped out of his car near Tecumseh, Ont., to confront a man who was holding up a taxi driver. Renaud belted the robber so hard in the face that he broke his hand in the scuffle. Still, he managed to rescue the cab driver and make the arrest.

Although Renaud left the force in 1950 in a cloud of controversy over accusations that he failed to impose discipline on his department, there were those who treated him with respect. When he died of a heart attack in August 1957 while vacationing at Red Cedar Lake near Sturgeon Falls, then Deputy Chief John J. Mahoney said, "He was a good policeman, a good detective. He was one of the best inspectors of detectives we have had. He was a good worker and a very active man. I certainly had a lot of respect for Claude Renaud, he was tops."

8
Troubleshooter
The Story of Carl Farrow
1951 – 1968

It has been suggested that had he not been the victim of a pickpocket, Carl Farrow might never have become a policeman. He was 16 when he headed west to harvest wheat and build grain elevators. He had saved $500, but made the mistake of carrying it with him, and one day when stopping in Winnipeg to have his picture taken, a female photographer spent an inordinate amount of time straightening up his suit in preparation to take his picture. He only learned afterwards that somehow she had slipped the money out of his pocket. Arguing with the owner of the establishment resulted in nothing but threats. And so, with only three cents and a rail ticket, a distraught, disappointed but proud young Farrow continued to Toronto, without eating. He refused to beg, or borrow in order to get a meal.

He told a *Star* reporter much later that it was that experience which made him "more determined than ever to be a policeman . . . I felt I could do some good as a police officer."

Sandwich East Inspector Bickford
with a would-be fisherman on a
school day. Truancy enforcement
was one of many police duties.
26 October, 1957. ws.

Carleton Wolsely Farrow, born in Cowansville, Quebec on March 6, 1903, was a tough-talking, intractable, tenacious, hulking six-foot-three man when he found himself at the helm of a police department that for years had been shattered with scandal and controversy. He said, "I thought I could clean it up in three months – it took four years."

The funny thing was that in spite of the dissension in the ranks, and the troubles that had plagued the department, there were 80 applicants who wanted that challenge. Windsor – a haven for gambling, prostitution and blind pigs – had been headline news across the province and in parts of the U.S. Things were so bad here, Farrow said, that "the police (themselves) were directing traffic in the whorehouses . . ."

The troubles in Windsor didn't surprise Farrow. He had been stationed here during the Roaring Twenties where he warred with rumrunners and bootleggers. His name regularly punctuated the pages of the *Star* as he led swift, bold raids into blind pigs, overturned "stills"

Chief Carl Farrow. ws

in the far reaches of Essex county, and stole into roadhouses late at night to seize liquor and gambling earnings. One rounder told a *Border Cities Star* reporter, "Hey, he wasn't someone you'd want to mess with . . . A nice guy, but no nonsense! You knew where you stood with him – he'd give it to you straight!"

It was after the First World War that Farrow finally went into police work. He had been trained by the Royal Air Force. In 1922, he went out west to join the Mounties, and served with the force from 1922 to 1925. His duties there included guarding harvest trains that transported workers to the Prairies. He was also responsible for the establishment of the first police post in the remote Fort Rae, of the Northwest Territories.

Farrow quit the Mounties, mostly because he was irked by its rules about not being permitted to marry for 12 years. "I was at that age, you figured you would get married. I signed up for three years, and when I was finished, I felt it was useless to sign up for any more time." Farrow returned to Ontario, and found a job with General Motors in Oshawa where he stayed until 1927. "When I got punching the clock, and working on the line, I thought, hell, there's not much future here . . . And I liked police work. There was a certain amount of excitement and adventure, so I thought I'd go back."

Farrow chose, not the RCMP, but the Ontario Provincial Police and

Police Constables Phil Bistany and Syd Stuart caution Walter and Taras Senchuk on the dangers of playing with fluorescent lighting tubes, August 1950. ws.

remained with that force till 1951 when he was appointed chief of the Windsor Police.

As a provincial officer, Farrow made a name for himself in police circles. When stationed in Hamilton, he played a key role in the Evelyn Dick murder case. The body of John Dick, her husband, was found dismembered. When Farrow went to investigate, he turned up the body of a child entombed in a block of concrete in the attic of her home. Mrs. Dick was sentenced to life imprisonment for the child's murder, but the circumstances leading to the murder of John Dick were never unraveled.

In 1928 Farrow was assigned to Amherstburg. He stayed there until 1934 when he was dispatched to Brantford to clear up problems there. In reflection, it seemed wherever there were "troubled spots," Farrow was chosen to go in "and to do the cleanup."

In Essex County during the heady 1920s, Farrow roamed fearlessly,

conducting raids, smashing down bootlegging joints, pursuing bank robbers and tracking down murderers. He was involved in most of the big cases during Prohibition, including making a key arrest in the kidnapping of *Border Cities Star* photographer Horace Wild who had been down at the export docks shooting pictures of the villainous activities of the rumrunners. Wild had been followed, snatched and detained by the rumrunners; and his cameras and pictures seized. Farrow was also embroiled in the "Birth Scandal" controversy involving a woman from an affluent Harrow family who gave birth to her lover's child, and had him bury it in a chicken coop.

Farrow encountered Al Capone in those days at the Amherstburg export docks, but only engaged in a brief conversation with the gangster. As far as he was concerned Capone was simply following Canadian laws with respect to exporting liquor. Farrow told the *Star*, "A lot of people thought they (the liquor exporters) were running around with guns

Constable Best tries unsuccessfully to rouse "Sleepy", a puppy who found his way to the police department August 21, 1950. ws

Constables at drill in 1956. ws.

around their waist. When they came ashore they weren't looking for trouble."

In the Twenties, the tall, strict provincial cop used his own car – a 1926 Whippet – and was paid by the mile. He wasn't popular then, and knew why headquarters moved him. "It was for political reasons – it was decided I had better move; they (the politicians in Windsor and Essex County) complained I was a little too tough. They said I was driving business away."

Before coming to Windsor in the 1950s, Farrow had risen to the rank of inspector with the 60-man Peterborough detachment, and completed 24 years with the province's police force.

The tall, ramrod-straight Farrow was like a drill sergeant who threw fear into the ranks. No one gave it a second thought to tempt the new chief with a part of the action. "No, they stayed clear of me. They knew I was one tough sonofabitch!" Nonetheless, the pressure mounted to

Sgt. Robert Duncan shows Rookie Paul Linton how to sight a revolver, 1957. WS.

remove Farrow.

"For several years after I got here," Farrow pointed out, "there were people following me around, trying to get something on me . . . You know, to get me out of here. But I was a good boy."

One of Farrow's first tasks in taking over the Windsor Police Force on February 12, 1951 was making it known he wouldn't tolerate the past. He didn't believe in "firing" officers, or purging the rank and file of its misfits and unsavory types. "I just kind of suggested it to them that they could go," he said. As it turned out, several who had led raffish, unruly lives could see no point in working under him. The good times had come to an end. Others – veterans from the War – had the potential of being seasoned police officers, and simply needed discipline and order. That's what Farrow intended to bring.

"I laid down the law, and that was it," he said, and with that, Farrow commanded uncanny respect. Although he had believed the situation

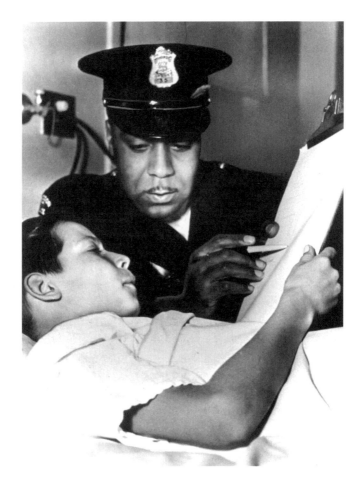

Constable Howard Watkins visits a
hit and run victim in order to
obtain details from the accident,
5 March 1959. ws.

would be cleaned up in three months – and it wasn't – there was no question of his "control" over the department.

Thus, the cleanup of the Border Cities began in earnest. Farrow put his new force into the task at hand – sending them in near-military style, into the fray of raiding gambling and bootlegging joints and rounding up pimps and prostitutes. He described the city as "a cesspool." In the annual report for 1950, however, there is virtually nothing about the changes. In the next year's report, Farrow detailed the actions of the "Special Investigations Branch" which operated under the command of Inspector John Burns. The special unit was formed in December 1950 under McNeill of the Ontario Provincial Police. In the past, it had been called the Morality Squad. It was Farrow, however, who mobilized these special officers into action.

Farrow provided this specialized division with 14 constables, a one-man hotel detail, and two sergeants. The team had at its disposal two

Burning the midnight oil. ws.

radio-equipped cars, and another without a radio. The unit provided coverage of the city 16 hours a day. His first attacks were on the bookie and betting establishments, and after a year, he contended that most had changed their mode of business to comply with provincial laws. Within a year, Farrow had also smashed the bawdy house business, but in doing so, had forced prostitutes into the streets to ply their trade in restaurants and hotels. To counteract this, Farrow demanded tougher laws.

In the course of his personal war, the new chief had put a number of blind pigs out of business. He sadly lamented that such places knew "no boundary and may appear at anytime, anywhere . . ."

Farrow worried over the spread of "the numbers racket" or "Policy Game," which he viewed as unique to Windsor. He said in the U.S., such a game had developed into the millions.

The Special Investigations Branch continued its vigilant skirmishes with lawbreakers for several more years, fanning out across the city,

Chief Carl Farrow. ws

cracking down on the bookmakers in billiard rooms, bowling alleys, dance halls, and tobacco shops. By 1953 Farrow had widened his scope to castigate youths using pin ball machines, devices which he considered "a menace" to kids.

That same year, Farrow expressed concern over the proliferation of "snack bars," in his view nothing more than "a rendezvous for teenagers and sometimes juveniles, and amongst them are irresponsible youths, both sexes, who due to lack of management and control are permitted to loiter and dance without any proper supervision." Farrow feared a diffusion of crime – perhaps to drinking, fighting, theft. His solution was plain: "It would appear that the elimination and prohibition of dancing, pin ball machines, juke boxes, and other devices of any similar nature or type would be of assistance in dealing with them." From the tone, it's evident Farrow wouldn't tolerate a broadening of crime. He demonstrated a rigid, arbitrary, circumspect and uncompromising attitude toward the cleanup of the city. As always, the new chief demonstrated displeasure with the present laws, and continued to press authorities for tighter controls.

By 1956 the special investigations unit, which had grown significantly over the years, began to scale down. For the first time since Farrow took over, his annual report betrayed optimism: "I feel the city is in very good shape as far as bootlegging, gambling and prostitution is concerned . . . The picture prior to 1951 was entirely different."

In those first years, the police department bulged at the seams in crowded facilities at the corner of Park and Goyeau – partly because the city and the county court rooms occupied the upstairs.

"There was no room at all. We had nothing here . . . As a matter of fact, if the detectives had someone in for questioning, they had to take them out to their cars parked out in the street. They had no room in the building. And nothing was confidential there – it was terrible."

Farrow saw the need for some fundamental changes in the police department. He modernized, bringing in proper telecommunications. More importantly, he established a system of "training" police officers. Till his appointment, the men were trained on the job, in the department itself. Farrow introduced his new system right away, dispatching recruits to be trained by the Ontario Provincial Police or the Royal Canadian Mounted Police. Later, he pressed for the creation of an Ontario police training centre. With the support of Judge Macdonald, the chief saw the establishment of the Ontario Police College at Aylmer in 1960.

In essence, in Farrow's time as Chief, he had transformed a coarse, scabrous, and ill-trained department into a crackerjack, formidable and modern police force. There is no exaggeration to the claim that his arrival brought out not only the shedding of that disreputable image, but really the first indications of the development of modern policing practices in the Windsor Police Force.

9

The Suburban Police Forces and Annexation

In January 1966, Windsor annexed five suburbs: Riverside, Ojibway, and portions of Sandwich East, West and South Townships. In doing so, its population increased by 50 per cent to 193,000, and by more than 300 per cent in land area to 50 square miles. The task that faced the Windsor Police involved the absorption of the suburbs' policemen, finding out how many more ought to be hired, nearly doubling the fleet of patrol cars, sorting out seniority and promotion problems, and shipping new

Riverside Police Chief Bryce Monaghan (left) demonstrates radar equipment for Gordon Stewart, Mayor of Riverside (centre), and Ronald Beasley, Chairman of the Riverside Police Commission. 15 June, 1961. ws.

The Sandwich East Police Department, 1954. ws.

recruits off to Ontario Police College.

Chief Farrow faced this new challenge when he was 64. He took it all in stride, telling the *Detroit News:* "Policemen, more than any other government people, are trained to accept the unexpected emergency – murders, bank robbery, tornado and that sort of thing, you know – as a routine way of life."

The Windsor Police Force grew immediately from 245 men to 377 with annexation. This included 29 civilian clerks. Newspaper advertisements and window placards immediately put out the request for new recruits. The department's goal was to add 45 new constables, aged 19 through 30 years, and 10 police cadets, age 17 and 18.

Salaries rose with annexation to $6,300 annually for a constable, plus $400 in longevity bonus for senior men, making the Windsor Police Force's pay scale second only to Toronto's. At the time, a Detroit senior patrolman was receiving $7,335 base pay, plus $300 for longevity.

Farrow faced dissatisfaction. There were 40 resignations over two years. The reasons listed, according to a civilian board of inquiry, were inadequate salaries, lack of public support for police work and "internal problems," such as an increased emphasis upon military-style discipline. Farrow never disguised the fact there were difficulties. In his 1966 report he maintained that morale remained "at a desirable level" despite the fact that 22 constables had been charged under the Police Act, Code of Offences against discipline.

It wasn't until the end of 1966 that Farrow realized how difficult a transition it was. In his annual report that year, it was evident that the traffic bylaws, licencing, traffic direction and enforcement all posed "major problems." For one, gasoline dealers objected to the enforcement of the closing time bylaw, with the result that amendments were made to permit the former Township gasoline stations to remain open as they had. Windsor stations as a result were allowed to stay open till 9 p.m. Thursdays through Saturdays. A canvassing of all licenced premises had to be conducted to ensure businesses complied with Windsor's bylaws.

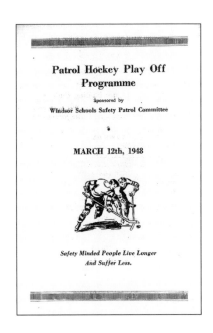

Patrol Hockey Play Off Programme. Municipal Archives, Windsor Public Library.

Safe Streets

The Safety Patrol

The first safety patrol programs in Canada were started by the Windsor Police in Windsor schools in 1938 under Chief Claude Renaud. In his annual report that year, the chief stated that it was formed "to cope with the menace of traffic accidents to children." The police department

Windsor Safety Patrols car ca. 1938.
ws

Early Windsor Police Patrol Wagon.
Windsor Police Service Museum

introduced the program in March 1938 after meeting with both the Windsor Separate School Board and the Windsor Board of Education. A committee was set up that included City Controller F. Begley, Trustees P. McCallum and E. W. Morris, Superintendent Campbell and Inspector Davidson of the Public Schools; Trustee Deziel, Inspectors Meladey and LaPlante of the Separate School Board, Harry Gignac, lawyer, and Chief Inspector W. H. Neale and Chief Renaud.

The safety patrols mobilized 550 boys and four girls. They were provided with Sam Browne belts and rain capes, paid for by voluntary subscriptions from merchants, and a grant of $400 from the Public School Board. Both school boards fielded a hockey team and held play-offs as an annual event.

Under Chief Farrow the Windsor Police formed its first unit of adult safety patrols. This was done in May 1951 to give protection to school children crossing busy intersections on their way to and from school. The department hired 20 men and seven women for its Adult Patrol.

Constable Edward Moreland shows school children the rules of traffic safety with Elmer the Safety Elephant and "Mr. Beep", a caricature car. 13 August, 1963. ws

Elmer The Safety Elephant

"Elmer The Safety Elephant" was first introduced to Windsor schools in September 1955 at St. Angela School through the cooperation of the Windsor Safety Patrol Association and the Sertoma Club of Windsor. In subsequent visits to 39 schools throughout the city, 19,270 pupils were introduced to the teachings of Elmer.

The program was shown to several Home and School Associations and Parent-Teacher Associations throughout the city and county. Radio Stations in Windsor and Leamington also broadcast the program.

Judge Bruce J. S. Macdonald negotitates on behalf of the Board of Commissioners of Police with the Windsor Police Association, 3 February, 1967. From left: His Honour, Judge Macdonald, WPA representatives John Garswood and Larry Langlois, and Chief Carl Farrow. ws.

10
The "Bejesus" Judge – The Story of Bruce J. S. Macdonald

The one thing he liked to tell people was that somehow through it all – through all the controversy and mayhem in the courts that marked his long career – he always managed "to land on his feet every time." When he stepped down from the bench at 75, Bruce J. S. Macdonald, or "Bejesus," as he was called, could look back at involvement in law that spanned more than 50 years. Among his accomplishments, he could count a private practice, a city solicitor, a war crimes prosecutor, Crown Attorney, the first head of the Ontario Police Commission, a member of various municipal police commissions, including Windsor's, and a judge for 16 years.

Once in an interview with the *Windsor Star*, he joked, too, that he had also managed to survive a heart attack and being struck down by a car. He also survived a fire bombing of his house in 1975.

Born in Rose Bay, Nova Scotia, Macdonald moved to Medicine Hat, Alberta where he attended the University of Alberta and received his B.A. and L.L.B. He spent a year at Harvard Law School for further law studies, and upon completion joined Windsor lawyers Gordon Fraser and Norman McLarty. McLarty later became a Liberal Cabinet minister in Mackenzie King's Government.

In 1930, Macdonald was hired as a full time city solicitor in Windsor.

This photograph ran on 22 January, 1964 with the exclamation "Well! Well!" ws.

Prior to that, solicitors had been hired either as part time or a contract basis. Macdonald's appointment made him the city's first solicitor, and in that capacity worked closely with Mayor David Croll and others during the Great Depression. He also saw the city through its amalgamation process, handling all the legal matters that brought Sandwich, Walkerville, East Windsor and Windsor under one jurisdiction in 1935.

The first controversy surrounding Macdonald occurred when he represented Windsor in a lengthy case over the restructuring of its debenture debt in front of the Ontario Municipal Board in 1937. Although he was legally entitled to "costs" associated with the case, Macdonald was sharply criticized for not returning these funds to the city. On such grounds, he was dismissed as city solicitor. One of the members of the Board of Control agitating for this action was someone who would become his adversary later in the 1940s. This was Arthur Reaume.

Bruce Macdonald. ws

    Macdonald returned to private practice. He married Norma Millard in 1939, and that September volunteered for active service with the Essex Scottish Regiment. He went overseas with the rank of major in July 1940. In 1942, he was back in Canada working as a training officer at Listowel. He returned to the Regiment after Dieppe as Lieutenant Colonel, and began the task of rebuilding its force. As the commanding officer of the unit during its ill-fated Normandy sortie at Ifs in 1944, Macdonald was held responsible for the Regiment's losses. He was promptly relieved of command.

    Macdonald rebounded once again, this time being appointed as a Canadian representative to the international investigation of German War Crimes at Supreme Headquarters Allied Expeditionary Force in 1944. Another Canadian involved in this unit was Clarence Campbell, whose name would later come to be associated with the National Hockey League.

Bruce Macdonald is sworn in as Essex County's new crown attorney by Judge A. J. Gordon in 1951, and takes a seat on the Windsor Police Commission. ws.

Macdonald's responsibility was crimes against Canadian service personnel. His most famous case was the prosecution of Major General Kurt Meyer, a German commander in the field at Normandy, who had been accused of ordering the murder of 48 Canadian soldiers. In an interview once, Macdonald recalled that during the trial in Aurich, Germany, Meyer had "a very dominating personality." He glared at Macdonald each time a question was put to him, and when he responded, it was done in a theatrical, intimidating and menacing way. Macdonald said the effect upon him was almost "hypnotic." It was only after he gathered enough courage and warned Meyer that he wouldn't be cowed by him that Meyer relented and accepted his fate.

Meyer eventually was convicted and sentenced to be shot. His sentence was commuted to life imprisonment, but he spent only nine years in New Brunswick's Dorchester Penitentiary before being paroled. Meyer returned to Germany and died in the 1970s.

Judge Bruce J. S. Macdonald's home was fire bombed in late fall, 1975. One of the perils of being a County Court judge and chairman of the Windsor Board of Commissioners of Police. ws.

When he returned from the war, Macdonald resumed private practice. Some say that he learned from that experience at the War Crime Trials to be the skilled and adroit interrogator, who could pull apart the most convoluted and clever tactics. When he returned, he found himself drawn into the political field, once again encountering his old foe, Arthur Reaume. Macdonald oversaw the 1948 inquiry into the affairs of Metropolitan Hospital. Suggested improprieties by Reaume, who was then mayor, did not hurt the suave and shrewd politician. He never seemed to lose his popularity with Windsor voters.

Three years later Macdonald stepped once again into controversy, this time involving charges of corruption against the Windsor Police and Chief Claude Renaud. With the resignation of the Crown Attorney, Macdonald was invited to assume the position in a city that the Attorney General of Ontario described as "the toughest assignment" in the province.

Those first years were strenuous on Macdonald, mostly because he also served on the city's police commission where he worked alongside Reaume. Some believed that Macdonald shouldn't have served on both, because his presence on the Commission might conflict with his work as the Crown Attorney. Macdonald shrugged off the criticism, and continued to serve on the Commission.

There was no question that the police department had been lax and inefficient in those years when Renaud was at the helm. Macdonald maintained he often sent police reports back for more thorough investigations. He was also forced to make several "unpleasant decisions" when it came to enforcing the law, particularly because they involved several prominent Windsor citizens who were involved in gambling and drinking.

In 1961 Macdonald was made a County Court judge, and was named chairman of the Ontario Police Commission (OPC). During his three-year tenure at the head of the OPC, he, along with Chief Carl Farrow, pioneered the way for the creation of the Ontario Police College in Aylmer. He was also responsible for the release of the OPC's report on organized crime in Ontario, which advocated a widening of police powers in a bill that was set to pass in 1963. The legislation was shelved instead in favor of civil liberties. There was no doubt that government legislators feared a dramatic increase in police powers through changes in the Police Act. It is believed that Macdonald was not asked to serve again on the Commission because he authored most of those recommendations.

Macdonald said the report, which was "so hot it never has been printed," contained contentious material, including confessions from Joe Valachi, the underworld apostate who was the first to speak out against the Mafia.

Macdonald defended the report vehemently, arguing that although some regarded it as "a manual" for a police state, it actually presented some "sound ideas" on how police activity could be regulated in Ontario. One such recommendation, for example, which has since been implemented, was drivers' licences carrying photographs of the owner. At the time, it was felt this would be an invasion of one's privacy.

Macdonald felt his work with the OPC helped bring about an upgrading of standards for policemen across Ontario, as well as increases in pay and benefits.

With respect to the Windsor Police Commission, he often boasted that while he served as one of its members – 26 years in all – the old scandals of the past, involving the police department, disappeared almost entirely.

Macdonald died at the age of 83 in June 1986.

"Sinjin" , the 1983 Police Dog. ws.

PART FOUR

Growth of the Windsor Police
1968 – 1992

Gordon Preston, Chief of Police
1968-1974. ws.

1
Police Chiefs

The Law and Order Man
Gordon Preston
1968–1974

When Robert Gordon Preston died in May 1974, Judge Gordon Stewart called him "the law and order man," but stressed that in setting the tone for his department, the emphasis had always been on fairness. Stewart, who was on the police commission at the time, described Preston as never being "unfair, harsh or cruel . . . He was a man who justifiably earned the respect of the men he led and this community."

Preston, a man slightly over six feet, who was born in Johannesburg, South Africa, joined the police department Nov. 1, 1937. Before that, he had been a machinist with the Ford Motor Company in Windsor. He didn't rise quickly in the ranks. It wasn't until 1951 that he was named patrol sergeant, then staff sergeant in 1954. Preston was appointed lieutenant in 1957, then six years later, inspector of the traffic division. The following year, Chief Farrow named him deputy chief. When Farrow resigned, Preston took over the department.

Marjorie Preston, widow of the late chief, remembers how devoted her husband was to his job. "He just loved being chief," she said, pointing out that it was a seven-day-a-week job. "He went down there every Saturday and Sunday."

Following Carl Farrow was a difficult task, said one former city official, because "Farrow was a tough, no-nonsense guy, and Preston was a pussycat." Judge Stewart agrees that Preston wasn't as vigorous a leader that his predecessor had been, "but then he never intended to be."

Preston, however, had the support of his department and the police commission. He also had a sterling record demonstrating concern for his own kind. As early as the 1940s, he was standing before the police commission arguing for a 40-hour, five-day-a-week job for his fellow constables. Policemen then were working a 48-hour week, and were allowed one day off in seven instead of the customary two.

Preston's record shows, too, that his time in the ranks gave him an inkling into the concerns and problems faced by the ordinary policeman. He was cited five times for his handling of criminal arrests, and he received a citation for outstanding achievement in the cause of highway safety. For 10 years he served as president of the Windsor School Safety Patrol Association. Preston was awarded a centennial medal for service to the community.

At the time of his death, the *Windsor Star* said the Windsor Police had

Officers ride bicycles in an effort to promote the 1972 Police Auction. WS.

"a reputation for fairness, a reflection of fair play that Chief Preston showed." The paper maintained that, "there was strength beneath the calm and gentle exterior that he showed the world, and quick-thinking energy beneath the calm with which he faced emergencies. His force reflects these qualities today, and Windsor should be grateful to his memory."

A Man of Calm & Good Sense
John Williamson
1974–80

He was someone who clearly cared about the rights of others, and someone who took the business of law enforcement seriously. At 58, when John McDowell Williamson retired as police chief, it was evident that he had made that impression.

The *Windsor Star* said that his leadership kept Windsor distant from "the wholesale lawlessness that once marred life in Detroit." The newspaper stressed that people in Windsor took that fact for granted, but Detroit visitors, accustomed to their city being called "Murder City U.S.A.," are always surprised by "the calm and order of Windsor."

The *Star* credited Williamson for that good reputation: "He will probably not want much fuss made over his retirement, but he deserves a great deal."

John Wlliamson, Chief of Police 1974-1980. Windsor Police Service.

Police from Windsor and Waterloo worked from August of 1968 until the following spring to crack the murder of a 70 year old night watchman with Walkerville Lumber Limited. His employer took all the detectives to dinner at Beach Grove Country Club. The investigation included twenty-nine detectives from both cities. 20 June, 1969. WS.

It was not hollow praise. Throughout his 35-year career as a police officer, Williamson – or "Willy," as he was known – stressed a kind of common sense approach to policing, and one that left the door open for communication, for compromise. Yet, Williamson wasn't about to bend the rules, to allow the kind of flexibility that would usher in a slackening of discipline.

Known as a shy, reserved man, John Williamson grew up on the west coast, the son of a fishing cannery manager. When he was 18, he joined the navy. During the Second World War, he was aboard the *HMCS Ottawa* when it was torpedoed by a German submarine. He was one of 34 survivors. He told the *Windsor Star* at the time of his appointment as chief that when he was out in the Atlantic – 900 miles from

One of the last call boxes in Windsor, at the southeast corner of University and Ouellette Avenues, before its removal in 1975. ws.

Newfoundland – he didn't have any doubt about his survival. It was a British Corvette that scooped him out of the water. He returned to Canada, to Windsor specifically, where he enrolled in an engine room course. It was there he met and married Doris Gaines in 1944.

In October 1945, he joined the Windsor Police. During his first year with the force, he was involved in the arrest of three men who attempted to break a safe at the former Kent Theatre on Ottawa Street near Moy. Williamson then was a probationary officer, and had only been with the force for 10 months.

He had been hired at a salary of $1,640 a year. Instead of a raise the following year, he was given "a new pair of boots." Williamson worked six days a week, getting two days off together about every two weeks.

Those first years with the force were difficult, since Windsor had been in the throes of bawdy houses and blind pigs, and it was difficult

Aikido demonstration at the 1977 Windsor Police Association's annual field day. ws.

enforcing the law when others were challenging it openly. It was also rough on the streets.

"We couldn't believe the conditions on the street. There was so much rowdiness." What bothered Williamson more was the impotence he felt in not being able to put a stop to illegal gambling, and the proliferation of prostitution and bootleg joints. He said that he, and many other policemen, who had come straight out of the service, were shocked to find the upper echelon of the force in support of such activities.

Williamson lasted only six weeks when he was placed on the old Morality Squad in 1949. Because he was determined to make convictions, he was thrown back on the street. Betting was wide open and was tolerated by the police. When he tried to point this out to his sergeant, his superior took him around to some of the pool rooms to show him that nothing of the kind was happening. Of course, these establishments were warned of their visits.

"But when I told them what I had seen, they took me off the squad and put me back on the street."

When Farrow took over, Williamson was an obvious choice for the newly-organized Morality Squad, now called the special investigations branch. They were so busy, said Williamson, that at one time, he had accumulated 20 convictions of blind pig operations before the court.

"It was hard work, but we had the support of everyone."

It didn't take Williamson long to climb the ladder. He was recognized

Members of the "Tactical Unit", formed in 1978. ws.

as a solid cop. By 1954 he was a patrol sergeant. Three years later he was working in the detective division. In 1961, Williamson was promoted to lieutenant, and was made the force's first personnel officer. It became his responsibility to deal with the 65 to 70 suburban police officers who joined the Windsor Police at the time of the merger in January 1966.

Williamson continued his education throughout his service with the

A total of 557 guns were melted down at the Ford of Canada foundry on 17 September, 1979. Most were handed in during the previous November's amnesty on dangerous weapons. ws.

force, taking courses in administration and police management at the Canadian Police College run by the RCMP in Ottawa.

In 1973 Williamson was named deputy chief, then in 1975 took over the department after Chief Preston's death. One of his first actions as chief was the appointment of a community services officer to handle any dealings with the press and work on crime prevention.

Williamson wasn't afraid to speak out when he was chief, and occasionally ran afoul of local lawyers, the newspaper, even Mayor Coleman Young's office in Detroit. A constant refrain of his was the leniency in the courts. He caused a furor over his swipes at the legal aid system. The chief had said that one or two previous criminal convictions should be grounds for denial of legal aid.

The *Windsor Star* angered Williamson when it reported a story based on what an anonymous caller gave to two reporters. The story involved Windsor police officers who had booked off sick to attend a party.

Chief Williamson stood his ground when Detroit Police wished to accompany Mayor Young on a visit to Windsor. He told the police department and the mayor's office that the Windsor Police would supply protection, and that armed policemen from Detroit would not

Officer Bill Hood checks out a darkened lot on robbery detail. 22 December, 1980. ws.

be tolerated in Windsor.

One of Williamson's main concerns actually was the influx of weapon-carrying Americans into Windsor. He ordered a crackdown at the border, making it clear to U.S. residents that police here would seize weapons and make arrests, if weapons of any kind – handguns, rifles or knives – were smuggled into Canada.

Among his accomplishments, Williamson added a new wing to the Windsor Police Station and opened up a new precinct station in the east end.

"A Cop's Cop"
Jack Shuttleworth
1981–84

When John Edward Shuttleworth came out of the Royal Canadian Air Force, he returned to Windsor in search of a job. He found one at the

Jack Shuttleworth, Chief of Police
1981-1984. Windsor Police Service.

Ford Motor Company working on the line. He had also put in his application at both the Windsor Police and the Windsor Fire Department. A month after he was accepted by the Windsor Police, he got a call from the fire department.

Jack Shuttleworth walked the old "race track" beat in those first years, a wide area that could be traversed twice in a night, if one didn't encounter any trouble in the hotels.

The training in those days for a policeman was "pretty nearly nil . . . The deputy chief would take you across the room and give you a copy of the Highway Traffic Act, and tell you a few city bylaws."

As far as a weapon, in those day, Shuttleworth didn't carry a revolver. He walked the beat with only a billy club.

The six-and-one-half foot Shuttleworth has always been known as a down-to-earth cop, or as the *Windsor Star* described him at the time of his appointment as police chief in 1981, "a cop's cop . . ." He survived the turbulent Fifties, witnessed vast changes that transformed the police department in the Sixties and Seventies, and came away with a recognition of a need for the return of some old values.

Visibility is one such value. Shuttleworth maintains that coupled with a rise in crime that has made police work far more time-consuming, officers now are burdened with more paper work, and time waiting for the court judgments. The overall effect is a distancing of the police officer from the public's eye, so that the only time one encounters a policeman is at the time of an arrest or handing out a traffic infraction.

"When I was chief, I used to make the time to go into the schools, if I were asked. That's what policemen should be doing. . . . The policeman today isn't in touch with the average citizen."

The old way of dealing out justice on the street, as it was between the 1940s and 1970s, may be frowned upon today, because of incidents of policemen abusing their authority. But there was a positive side, too, where policemen took the extra time to talk with these lawbreakers, in many cases, simply issuing strong warnings. At the base of these incidents, Shuttleworth contends, there was an effort made to connect with individuals, and to turn them away from crime.

Shuttleworth gives the example of a 10-year-old boy who had been caught shoplifting at the old Kresge store downtown:

> I said to the manager, "What do you want to do with him?" And he said he didn't really want to do anything . . . He just wanted the kid out of the store . . . So I said, "Okay, let me handle this." I took the kid outside and I told him to go home and get his parents and meet me at the police station in a half hour. And when we were done talking there, I told him to go with his parents back to the Kresge store and apologize to the manager . . . Now

Lost! Constable Kirk Mason asks, "Which way?" 12 May, 1982. ws.

the kid wasn't a bad kid, and the manager knew that . . . And when it was all done, everybody was happy. I don't think that kid ever did it again .

Shuttleworth knows the pressures facing the modern policeman. An officer faces expulsion if he lets his temper get the better of him. The urge to retaliate is "only human, and it's always there." Shuttleworth remembers an investigation at the Detroit Windsor Tunnel where someone he was arresting spit in his face. "Well, that's about all I could take," he said, but pointed out that instead of retaliating he went off to another room to wash his face and contain his anger.

"But when I first came on the force, you administered justice on the street corner," Shuttleworth said.

In doing so, there was more respect for the law. Officers took it upon themselves to send kids home to get their parents, thereby involving the family in the offense. In many instances, a good talking-to, Shuttleworth maintained, was all that an offender needed to curb breaking the law.

A plainclothes detective handcuffs a suspect following a mid-afternoon robbery attempt at the Ouellette and Riverside Bank of Commerce. 12 March, 1982. ws.

"I always felt that if you treated people half way decent, they'd respect you."

Shuttleworth said such regard even came from criminals. Once at the former British American Hotel downtown, he rushed in to break up a fight, and found an old safe cracker "who had been knocking off safes right left and centre all over town," coming to his rescue. "He was pulling these guys right off my back." The reason was that this man in the past had always been treated "with civility and respect" by Shuttleworth.

"I have always said that if that little guy grows up with respect for the law, then it will make your job (as a policeman) that much easier."

Shuttleworth's rise in the ranks of the Windsor Police was quick. The former basketball and football all-star, who attended Patterson

"Bank closed early today" was the sign on a Wyandotte Street East bank following a robbery on 17 August, 1982. ws.

Collegiate and Assumption, spent three and one half years walking a beat before being assigned to the old morality squad. He remained there until 1955. During his time with that unit, he was promoted to detective. In 1966, Shuttleworth was made acting Detective Sergeant. Eight years later, he was appointed Inspector. In 1976, he was made Staff Inspector, followed by his appointment as deputy chief in 1980, and finally, chief in October 1981.

At the time, *Windsor Star* police reporter Michael Frezell wrote that when people who knew Shuttleworth described him, "it's in terms of a quiet man, one difficult to know. They also speak of respect, something he gets and gives."

When Shuttleworth kept his promise and resigned at the age of 60,

Constable Frank Garbutt carries a parcel suspected of being a bomb out of the Simpsons, Limited store on 14 March, 1982. ws.

many city officials were unhappy to see him go. Mayor Elizabeth Kishkon praised him for his "honesty and fairness."

The former police chief likes to think of himself as that, having survived those terrible years of the 1940s and 1950s when the police department's credibility was shattered. He remarks, "I always tell people I may not have been the smartest, but I was honest." He maintained that it was a principle he seemed to follow, and applied to everyone he encountered in police business.

Shuttleworth said if a policeman was brought up on charges, he would back him to the end if there was even the slightest shred of evidence of innocence. "But if a policeman got in trouble, and he was wrong, then he was out. I wouldn't tolerate that!"

In his short term as chief, Shuttleworth didn't disturb the patterns of the past, although he continued to restructure the force as had been started by his predecessors. He also introduced the two-channel radio systems for the department, and saw the old filing systems being displaced by computers.

In its editorial at the time of his retirement, The *Windsor Star* characterized Shuttleworth as "tough but sensitive..." The newspaper noted that while he had been named chief in the midst of a recession in the city, he managed to keep things under control and "provide the service Windsor had come to expect of an efficient, well-run force."

Fighting the Las Vegas of the North
Chief John Hughes
1984–1988

He called his men "the blue soldiers." He'd say they were "the main people" within the force. Such an attitude came out of a deep involvement on the street. When he took over the chief's job, April 1, "April Fool's Day," in 1984, he told *The Star* that he missed being on that beat.

Hughes was born and raised in Windsor. Like so many others after the war, he returned to his home looking for a job, and found one with the Windsor Police which seemed eager to hire servicemen. Hughes had spent the war, and two years following it in the U.S. Air Force . In June 1949 he joined the Windsor Police. From that time to his retirement he served in just about every rank, from the patrol division and traffic divisions to special investigation and criminal sections. He was appointed to work in the youth branch of the force in 1960, then was promoted to head it in 1966, and remained in charge till 1974. Within the first six months of 1974, Hughes was made an inspector. He went from duty inspector in charge of police operations 24 hours a day, to being in charge of police equipment and teaching new officers. Hughes became the first community service officer for the Windsor Police in 1974 when Williamson took over the department. In that job, Hughes started one of the force's first crime prevention programs.

John Hughes, Chief of Police 1984-1988. Windsor Police Service.

In February 1976, Hughes was promoted to staff inspector in the traffic division. In June 1980, Hughes was appointed deputy chief. Four years later, he was named chief. In 1987, Hughes became president of the Ontario Association of Chiefs of Police.

In those first years as a policeman, Hughes established himself quickly. In June 1950, just a rookie, he managed to save a man and halt the spread of a fire that might have caused an explosion. He had been at the Bruce Avenue call box when he saw a man – his hair, face and upper body engulfed in flames – run from a nearby building. Hughes grabbed the man and beat down the flames. After calling an ambulance, he rushed into the basement of the building, and with a hand fire extinguisher, put out the fire before it spread to some highly volatile cleaning fluids in an adjacent room.

In 1959, Hughes was in the paper again – this time for saving the life of a 21-year-old woman who plunged into the Detroit River to attempt suicide.

Two other events stand out: the time Hughes worked three days straight after the explosion at the Metropolitan Store downtown when 10 people were killed; the other, his investigation of the brutal murder of six-year-old Ljubica Topic of Drouillard Road in May 1971.

Two officers prepare to enter a
suspect's residence. 28 February,
1987. ws.

As chief, Hughes was outspoken and opinionated. Still he tried to
bring a level of common sense to decisions. His targets were the
concerns of most – for justice, for decency. It was during his tenure that
the strip clubs began to spring up. Hughes waged an indefatigable battle
to put them out of business, but ran up against loopholes in the law. He
went after drunk drivers with a vengeance, warning violators would be
caught and prosecuted. He helped establish a Windsor chapter of
M.A.D.D. or Mothers Against Drunk Driving.

Hughes publicly worried, too, about the spread of violence in the
city, noting that in 1985 how terrible and shocking it was to see a 31-year-
old woman with her two children dying in a fire that was deliberately set.

That same year, a school teacher was slain and his wife seriously
wounded by armed intruders who forced their way into the couple's
house. Hughes demonstrated, too, that he wouldn't tolerate "an excessive force" by the Windsor Police in its arrests. He disciplined members

Constable Bert Rieti involed in the
1985 apprehension of a suspect. ws

of his own department for such abuse of power. He also let it be known
that although there had been as high as 65 complaints of abuse about
police from citizens in 1984, 58 officers missed work and collected
compensation that same year because they were injured when making
arrests.

In an article in the *Windsor Star* in March 1984, Hughes acknowl-
edged that he enjoyed being a street cop, but those days did take their toll
on him. It was difficult coming face to face with elements of society that
police commonly label "scum," "creep," and "rounders."

Hughes often maintained that police officers took the attitude they
treated criminals the way they were treated: "They would tell me, 'If they
come on strong to me, I'm going to come on strong to them.'" Hughes
pointed out to the *Star* how at one time, he, himself, had to "overcome"
such attitudes.

"I had to make up my mind a long time ago that people would not
dictate to me how I'm going to react."

Minutes after this 13 July, 1988 photograph was taken , a disturbance involving knives led to two arrests on the spot by Constable Mike Lenehan. ws.

Hughes' sincerity was rarely doubted. One of his last major addresses before his death in 1989 was to the Ontario Police College graduation ceremonies in July 1988. He told rookie officers that when they returned to their police departments, they ought to expect to work for "some (officers) who have no integrity whatsoever . . ." Hughes stressed that integrity was "the intellectual wholeness of the police officer." That meant avoiding the pitfalls of being "a bully," "a fence sitter," or "a liar."

Challenging the Future
Without Losing the Values of the Past
Chief Jim Adkin

When he was five years old, he sat in his father's police cruiser during a parade in Tilbury, Ont., and knew then that when he grew up he would be a policeman.

"It was a dream fulfilled 14 years later," Jim Adkin said, pointing out that when he got out of high school, he joined The Windsor Police. That

October in 1961, he turned up at the department downtown — it was only a day after his 19th birthday.

Today, Jim Adkin is the police chief in Windsor. He succeeded John Hughes as the eighth police chief since amalgamation.

"I was very proud of my dad, and what he did." Throughout his childhood, whenever someone was needed to play the role of the police officer, Adkin always jumped at the chance.

"It's what I had always wanted to be."

This regard for his father was so strong, said Adkin, who was born in Chatham in 1942, that when his father passed away, he yearned to follow in his father's footsteps by taking over his father's old job. His father, who had served as an Ontario Provincial Police Officer, later went to the New York Central Railway Police. It was a good thing, Adkin said, that he didn't take the job, because six months after it was offered, the position was eliminated.

Instead, Adkin remained with the Windsor Police. He joined as a cadet in 1961. By 1963, after attending Ontario Police College, he was a constable. In his years with the force, Adkin worked in patrol, traffic, the special investigations branch and the drug squad.

James Adkin, appointed Chief of Police in 1988.

Those early years were "tough," and police constantly were challenged on the street. "There were some really tough dudes then," noted Adkin, who confessed it was not at all uncommon for a policeman to go head to head with these rounders.

Adkin is sorry to see those times have vanished, because there was "a simplicity" to the law then. Gone is an approach to police work that somehow made perfect sense. "It's too bad it's changed, because in those days you might come across a kid who had broken into a building, and instead of taking him downtown, you might bring him to his parents. And ninety-nine per cent of the time if the parents dealt with this boy, it was better.

"I wonder about how many kids we saved by taking this informal approach to justice!"

Today when prospective candidates are examined, Adkin said first and foremost is whether or not these individuals have "sensitivity."

The police chief is buoyed up by correspondence about how officers have taken a few extra steps to ensure a citizen's well-being. This was the case after one break-in where the investigating constable took the time to telephone the homeowner the following day simply to check if he could be of assistance.

It is because of this sort of action that Adkin saw the need for the force to adopt a new name that would reflect the true involvement of the department in the community. The Windsor Police changed its name to Windsor Police Service in 1989. Adkin puts it simply: "It's exactly what we do! We provide a service."

Windsor's R.I.D.E. (Reduce
Impaired Driving Everywhere)
program on Ouellette Avenue, 28
December, 1990. ws.

The truth is, Chief Adkin points out in that characteristically soft-spoken, patient voice, twenty per cent of the calls received by the Windsor Police are crime related, while the balance is tied to "service," or work with people who find themselves in difficult straits.

"We are more than a law enforcement agency," Adkin maintains.

What he would like to see is a higher profile of the department, and part of that can be achieved by a greater concentration in the schools.

He is optimistic about the future, but stresses the need for better technology. To that end, Adkin plans to update the investigative branch. He also envisions a new police station in the downtown, and thinks that a museum housed there would achieve part of that goal to make the police more visible in the community.

Adkin faces the challenge of what legalized gambling will bring to Windsor. He has already stressed that his endorsement of the city's proposal is hinged on two factors: the provincial government must own and operate these gambling establishments, and it must provide not only its own policing within these places, but increased personnel on the Windsor Police to meet the demands that could spin off from this activity.

Adkin expects there will be "challenges" to the laws from the underworld: "They will test the waters, and we have to be ready for that." If the Windsor Police Service is understaffed, there could be a spread of prostitution, bootlegging and illegal gambling.

"I think we can keep things clean," said Adkin, but it is going to mean being "tough" on even the slightest hint at crime. Windsor has met this challenge before. Adkin recalls that when he came on the force in the

1960s, motorcycle gangs threatened to take up residence in the city. The police made it clear these gang members were not welcome here.

Adkin said what is often forgotten by the community is that it is the people within the community who set the tone. "The community will determine what kind of laws we should have, and the police are left to enforce them."

The police tread a delicate path in not setting itself up as "the moral judge" of the community.

2
Pipers

The Windsor Police Pipe Band has flourished since its inception in 1967. In November 1967, the executive of the Windsor Police Association was asked by then Constable John Burrows for support in starting the pipe band.

The association named Sgt. Cal Allison as liaison officer for the band, the police department and the association. In those first years, the band practised at the City Market Building, the Windsor Armouries and the HMCS Hunter Building. It made its first public appearance at the Annual Inspection and Field Day in 1969. The band is now under the direction of the Windsor Police Service.

3
The Border Problem

The border still poses a problem. From the days of Alexander Bartlet to the present, there has been a fear of living on the border. In the 19th century, the threat of a Fenian invasion left people shaking in their boots. In the Roaring Twenties, stories of gangsters roaming the streets, and newspaper accounts of shootings on the Detroit River or in downtown hotels caused many to cower in fear. In the Fifties, organized crime sent shivers and shock waves through the city. Today those threats still exist. And police chiefs come and go, complaining about the spread of crime. Often it centres on the issue of gun control. Despite signs posted clearly at the border, Americans continue to bring in weapons.

It is not uncommon for police to seize more than 100 weapons a year at the border. Windsor has also become a major smuggler of narcotics, especially LSD and marijuana. And usually this brings in a violent element.

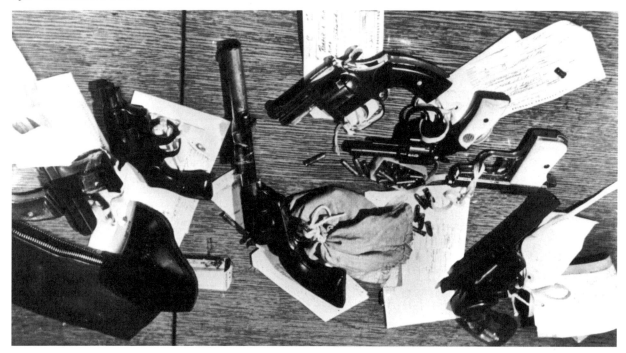

The guns seized from Baptist ministers in September of 1981. ws.

Occasionally, it brings in another sort of crowd. Fourteen Baptist ministers in 1981, attending a convention in Detroit, decided to cross the border to get a glimpse of Canada. They were promptly arrested. They carried, not Bibles and religious tracts, but lethal weapons – not modest and discrete handguns, but restricted arms, ranging from .357 caliber Magnums to .22 caliber revolvers. The newspapers sarcastically called this Canada's 11th commandment: Thou Shalt Not Carry Guns! Eric Mayne of the *Windsor Star* mockingly wrote, "Praise the Lord and pass the ammunition!"

But such an occurrence was not so uncommon. A Windsor police officer confided to a reporter that one night he removed a gun from a 70-year-old man from the southern U.S.

The policeman said, "I asked him why he needed a gun and he told me, 'If the people in my neighborhood know I don't have a gun in my house, they'll break in, rob my possessions and rape my wife. That's why.'"

4
Crime Stoppers

In April 1985, the Windsor Police embarked on the Crime Stoppers program. the *Windsor Star* lauded the move, pointing out in its editorials that citizens of the city would gladly throw their full support behind the police in this move.

The program is designed to encourage people, through an anonymous witness plan, to provide police with information leading to the arrest of criminal suspects as well as the recovery of stolen property. Cash rewards up to $2,000 were offered from the outset.

The first Canadian Crime Stoppers program was launched in Calgary in 1982. In three years, it proved successful, recovering more than $1.5 million worth of stolen goods. One lady even turned in her boyfriend so she could collect the reward. She confided to police, "I can always get another boyfriend, but I can't always get $200."

Hamilton was the first to introduce Crime Stoppers in Ontario in 1983.

In its first year of operation in Windsor, Crime Stoppers solved 271 cases and made 121 arrests. Information received through the organization also helped police recover $236,241 in stolen property, and led to the seizure of $105,350 in illicit narcotics. In return, the police program paid out $11,420 in rewards for anonymous information.

5

Women In Blue

Women figured in the operation of the Windsor Police from the very beginning when the department employed matrons. It wasn't until the 1970s, however, that women were hired as constables. The Windsor Police followed the lead of other forces in the country. The Ontario Provincial Police and metropolitan forces in Toronto, Hamilton and Ottawa had trained and hired female constables.

It was Chief John Williamson in 1975 who decided it was time to hire women. At that time, he remarked, "In these days of women's lib the ladies feel they can do the same job as men."

The chief admitted the force had always been reluctant to hire women, because it was felt by the police administration that women were not physically capable of carrying out all the functions demanded of a police officer.

"That's all changing," Williamson told *The Star*.

Indeed, it has. Today, there are 21 female police constables, one sergeant and six cadets.

The first women officers on the Windsor Police were Lisabeth Taylor, then 27, and Elizabeth Tuz, 22. Taylor had been a secretary, and Tuz, a waitress. They were hired in July 1975, and were sent to the Ontario Police College for training. At the time, Taylor told *The Star*, "Some of

Windsor's first female constables -
Liz Tuz (left) and Lisabeth Taylor.
31 December, 1975. ws.

my brothers were leery of the idea. They feel it's a man's job. And one of my friends wanted to know if I had a mean streak."

Minimum requirements for female candidates set down by the Windsor Police in 1975 called for women to be at least five feet, four inches tall and weigh a minimum of 120 pounds. Males must be five feet, eight inches tall, and weigh at least 160 pounds.

Williamson was quick to point out in 1975 that he wouldn't tolerate a situation in Windsor where male officers would try and protect female constables in situations that were potentially dangerous – simply because they were women. He told the press, "If officers have to protect fellow officers, they can't devote all their energies to the job at hand."

Ironically, when the Windsor Police Commission approved the hiring of female constables, and introduced further regulations regarding the dress and hair styles of officers, inadvertently it may have neglected to address these to the female officers. The Commission stated that uniformed members should be "properly shaved except that a neatly trimmed mustache may be allowed, which shall not extend beyond the corners of the mouth. The spikes on a waxed mustache shall not exceed one inch in length. The hair on the head shall be cut tapering downward to no closer than one inch above the shirt collar . . ."

6
Man With A Record

Most policemen, who have been on the Windsor force for any great length of time, remember Yorky. The mere mention of the name brings smiles and a flood of stories.

Yorky was no policeman, no hero. He was someone with a big thirst, a warm smile, a good nature. His claim to fame was coming ever so close to breaking the Guinness Book of Records for drinking offenses. At one point, lawyers, judges and police officials here lobbied to get him into the record books. Windsor lawyer Frank Montello led the way, trying to make the case that Yorky's 700 convictions might have been some kind of achievement.

When Norman Haworth died at 94 in November 1984 his funeral was front page news in the *Windsor Star*. Journalist Paul Vasey, who had befriended the British-born man years before, and wrote extensively about him, described this curious figure as "a little man with a large legend."

At the funeral were people with whom Yorky was forever tangling. Judge Stewart, who had often described his old buddy, as "a class guy," sat in the front pew, having taken off his 68th birthday to honor the man who so often had disrupted his courtroom. Beside him was Montello who had defended this colorful character so many times he no longer remembered the number. Both had promised Yorky they would be his pallbearers. And they were there to oblige him.

The stories of Yorky are legion. There is no exaggeration to the fact that he listed the Windsor Jail as his mailing address, and that when he was there, his jailers rarely locked his cell. Yorky may be the only prisoner in the history of the jail for whom the staff baked a cake and threw a birthday party. He cleverly managed to get the courts on his side, so that the lockup became a kind of second home, a halfway house — at least until he got his pension cheque. Often that monthly cheque was deposited with the liquor store where some of his cronies believed he had "a charge account." That was because he'd wink at the staff at the liquor outlet and remark, "Put it on my bill!"

The best story, of course, was when Yorky climbed the CKLW-TV

Constables Jerry Maisonville and James Weston lead Norman "Yorky" Haworth to a "new stay in the pokey". 20 June, 1956. ws.

tower on a $2 bet in 1956. He had just been let out of the Windsor Police lockup. The city magistrate's court had given him time to pay a fine for intoxication. Apparently in a mood to celebrate, but also on a dare, Yorky decided to slip into the TV compound at about 3 p.m., and climb the tower to the top.

York managed to climb 60 feet before a Windsor police officer persuaded him to return to the ground.

While he may have been a nuisance to the Windsor Police, he was treated with respect, because, he had regard for officers, lawyers and judges. Stewart remembers Yorky's visits to his office each Christmas. He'd sit across from the judge and write out a Christmas card and hand it to him.

At the time of Yorky's death, Judge Stewart pointed out, "I'm not saying goodbye to one of my favorite characters. I'm saying goodbye to one of my favorite friends."

7

The Royal Bank Heist

At that time, it was the biggest "cash robbery" heist of a bank in Canadian history. It took place on a Saturday — when banks weren't open. Although police nabbed the bandits, they never managed to recover all the money that was stolen. As a matter of fact, only a little more than $100,000 of the estimated $1.1 million was found.

This daring, and to some extent, ingenious robbery took place Dec. 18, 1971 in the heart of downtown at the Royal Bank at Pitt and Ouellette.

Unknown to the Windsor Police then was the arrangement the bank had with the Windsor Raceway to count and confirm deposits on Saturdays. Each night at the end of the races, an armored car transferred money to Ryan Security in Detroit for safekeeping. The next morning, the car would bring the money to the Royal Bank to be counted. While police had no knowledge of this, for some reason the bandits did. And thus, instead of trying to "hit" the raceway, and encountering all sorts of risks, the target for the bankrobbers became the bank.

It is still uncertain how these thieves pulled off the heist. Indeed, there are many questions unanswered. Did they have keys to the bank? From evidence given later at the trial, it seems one of the robbers had been reading up on locksmithing, but when could the keys have been made? And if they used keys, then how did they get inside? Perhaps an "inside" source assisted them? The only access to the sealed "counting room" where the money was being sorted was with the use of a key or by an internal push-button system. And how did the five escape the notice

Chained suspects in the 1971 Royal Bank robbery are led from the paddywagon to jail. ws.

of everyone while they were casing the bank for months preceding the heist? And what happened to the "getaway car?" — it was never found. And why on the night before the robbery did one of the robbers offer a ride to a 19-year-old male hitchhiker on Ouellette Avenue, and make a pass at him? Of course, the most pressing query is what happened to the rest of the money? Why hasn't it turned up yet?

The cast of characters involved in the robbery story were George Ivan Davison (a master safecracker), William Ferguson, Donald Patrick Derosie, James Ernest MacArthur (a trainer and breeder of horses), and Neil Garrington, and Edna Helen Lefebvre. Ferguson was certainly not the perfect choice. He was so fat that one witness recalled him at the Holiday Inn in Windsor after the robbery. She said he was so big that he "practically filled the door." Davison reminded other Holiday Inn personnel of actor Alan Ladd.

It is still unclear how many were involved at the actual scene of the crime. Some witnesses contend there were four; others indicate five. In any case, on the morning of Dec. 18 four or five gunmen entered the Pitt Street entrance of the bank en route to the "counting room." The four passed through two security doors. In the counting room were 12 women and one man. From evidence given later, it seems the bandits, carrying dufflebags and plastic wash pails, were familiar with the layout of the bank — they had been there before. The gunmen startled the 13 in the counting room, handcuffed them together and hooked them to a pole inside the men's washroom. Once this was accomplished, the robbers set about stuffing the $1.1 million into the dufflebags.

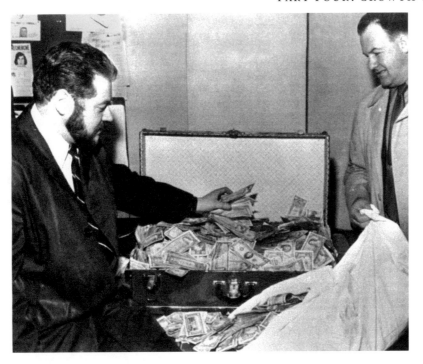

Although Detectives James Cole (left) and Richard Beith thought that they had recovered the entire sum of 1.1 million dollars, in reality they had only recovered $100,000. Much is left unexplained about the robbery. 21 December, 1971. ws.

During the heist, Bank Manager Kenneth Moore could not have chosen a worse time to pay a visit to the bank. As he stepped into the bank, he ran right into one of the gunmen. Moments later, the bank manager was handcuffed to the counting cage. It was until nearly an hour and a half after the robbery that Bruce Cornish, assistant manager, arrived and found his boss, and bank employees stranded — and the bank robbed.

The bank heist did not come as a surprise to the Metropolitan Toronto Police. For five months prior to the crime, the police there had been watching the five, anticipating that they were up to something. Upon their return of the five to Toronto, the police put a tail on the bandits. One man was followed to a hardware store where he bought a steamer trunk. In an effort to track the luggage, an undercover cop managed to put his initials on the trunk. Later when police raided a room the bandits rented at a Holiday Inn in Etobicoke, they found the piece of luggage brimming with money — but not all of it, only $147,716. Arrested were Ferguson, Derosie, Davison, Lefebvre and another woman who was released later.

MacArthur was arrested later in Montreal, and Garrington in Miami.

At the trial, Judge Bruce Macdonald promised lighter sentences in order to recover the balance of the money, but the bank robbers refused to cooperate. With that, Macdonald handed down stiff sentences to the accused. To this day, other than dribs and drabs found in the possession of these robbers, there is still nearly $1 million missing.

8
Heroes for Our Time
Uncle Al
Alton Parker

On one sheet of foolscap, badly-typed and crammed together, Alton Parker in 1975, five years after retiring from the Windsor Police Force, typed out, "This is my life." Simple, straightforward, modest. The document begins with his birth on Mercer Street in Windsor where his parents, Ida and Crawford Parker raised and looked after him. He doesn't say in it what day he was born on, but it was July 3, 1907. He does mention what he thinks important. His mom and dad's names – Ida and Crawford Parker. He also mentions the neighborhood – attending the old Mercer Street School, later Windsor Collegiate Institute, then Lowe Vocational. It was at night school that he earned a certificate in Diesel Engineering.

At 11, Parker says in this document that he "accepted Christ," and joined the First Baptist Church.

What he doesn't state immediately was what he was best remembered for. He leaves it for the end. The Kids' Party. Uncle Al's Kids' Party. It grew from a handful in 1966 – some two dozen kids – to in excess of 800. Years later, he used to boast that on the second Tuesday in August each year, it never rained. That every year at Erie and Howard, in the park, now called Alton C. Parker Park, the party would take place. Rain or shine. And for 22 consecutive years, the rain held.

What Parker also doesn't say in his one-page autobiography – or at least not right away – is something else he's best known for. Parker was Canada's first black detective.

Alton Parker joined the Windsor Police Force in 1942. He was the first black police officer to work here. The newspaper story announcing his appointment said he was the second "colored employee" to be hired by the Windsor Police Commission. The first was Charles Peterson who had worked in the police garage for 10 years before that.

And while Parker proved to be an outstanding policeman, he was the recipient of only one promotion in 28 years – as detective in 1953 when Chief Carl Farrow appointed him to that new position. From 1950s to 1970, Parker didn't advance any further. He worked in the property room for the last five years of his career.

Even so, he had great respect for the job, and for what it meant to be

The Windsor Star

So-Creditable
CLOUDY, SHOWERS
4 a.m. 56, 9 a.m. 58, 2 p.m. 68
Low tonight 54, high Saturday 72

FINAL
★ ★ ★ ★

VOL. 89, NO. 29   38 Pages   WINDSOR ONTARIO FRIDAY OCTOBER 5 1962   SEVEN CENTS

PAY COURIER ROBBED OF $7,000

Unruly Socred Keeps Talking; Sent From House

Speaker 'Names' Dumont After Early Flareup

OTTAWA—Social Credit M.P. Bernard Dumont, member for Bellechasse, was ejected from the Commons today when he refused to yield the floor to Speaker Marcel Lambert.

The rare step, which electrified the Commons as today's sitting began, was the harshest yet taken by Mr. Lambert in his continuing attempts to curb what he has labelled as breaches of the rules by the opposition and especially the 30-member Social Credit group.

Mr. Dumont was "named" by the Speaker—in effect, admonished—and ordered to leave the chamber.

When he at first gave no sign of heeding the Speaker's order, Mr. Lambert called for the sergeant-at-arms, Lieutenant-Colonel David V. Currie, the prelude to a forcible ejection.

But then Mr. Dumont picked up his papers from his desk and left voluntarily. His suspension lasts only for the rest of today's sitting, which ends

French Vote Battle Shapes Up

QUESTION COURIER—A payroll courier was robbed of about $7,000 this morning. The courier, Peter Groff, is shown, at right, indicating to Detective Sergeant Alton Parker the direction in which the two bandits drove off.

Federal Troops Released

Restless Peace in South

Bandit Grabs Cash Briefcase At Gunpoint

Police are questioning five suspects in connection with the armed holdup today of a payroll courier. About $7,000 was taken. The five were picked up in a restaurant in the area at about 1 p.m.

A payroll courier was robbed of about $7,000 shortly after 11 a.m. today when a gunman held a gun on him as he was parking his car while returning from the bank.

The gunman, his face covered with a black silk stocking, grabbed the courier's briefcase and forced him into the back seat of his car.

He then ran across the road to where an accomplice was waiting in a car and the two fled.

The money was the weekly payroll for Meretsky Bernstine and Meretsky Scrap dealers and Romeo Machine Shop, both located at 1577 Howard Ave.

The courier, Peter Groff, was on his way back from the Canadian Imperial Bank of Commerce at Aylmer and Wyandotte. Company officials said he picks the payroll up at approximately the same time every week. He is generally accompanied by another man, but was alone this time.

Giants Take Early Lead Over Rivals

Hiller Doubles, Comes Around For Quick Edge

SAN FRANCISCO (UPI)—Chuck Hiller doubled and came home on a sacrifice and an infield grounder in the first inning today to give the San Francisco Giants an early 1-0 lead over the New York Yankees in the second game of the World Series.

FIRST INNING

YANKEES: Hiller threw out Kubek. Pagan threw out Richardson. Tresh walked. Mantle popped to Pagan.

No runs, no hits, no errors, one left.

GIANTS: Hiller doubled down the right field line. F. Alou bunted and was retired by Long unassisted, Hiller going to third. M. Alou grounded out, Richardson to Long, Hiller scoring. Mays struck out.

One run, one hit, no errors, none left.

SECOND INNING

YANKEES: Maris walked on a 3 and 2 count. Berra hit into

Freshman In Politics New M.P.P.

Victory Brings Wintermeyer Call

---

a police officer. When his granddaughter Diane Steele was presented her police badge from the Peel Region Police Force, Parker told her that it stood for integrity, and never to abuse the privilege and trust the badge allowed.

Parker did serve as a member of the Board of Directors of the Windsor Police Association for three terms. His wife, Evelyn, joined the Women's Auxiliary (Policemen's Wives) and became president of the group.

Among the awards and honors – and there were many – Parker received both the Order of Canada Medal and the Ontario Medal for Good Citizenship in 1976, and the Queen's Silver Jubilee Medal the following year. In 1987, he received an honorary law degree from the University of Windsor, and the following year was named "Person of the Year" of the North American Black Historical Museum.

The awards surprised Parker. Even embarrassed him a little. Not that he didn't think he deserved them, but simply because he considered himself quite ordinary – not at all the extraordinary humanitarian. His work with children grew out of the devotion he had to his religion, his church.

Although Alton Parker's police work put him on the front page of The Windsor Star on 5 October, 1962, he is best remembered for a lifetime of community service. ws.

Detectives Alton Parker and Stanley Lossowski inspect materials for the 1966 police auction sale. ws.

A touching moment for Parker was when he was invested into the Order of Canada in 1976. Following the ceremony at Rideau Hall, a man approached him to shake his hand. He told Parker, "I'm so ashamed of myself that I never thanked you for not charging me that night in 1944. You scared me and I straightened out and continued with my education after that."

Parker told the story to *Windsor This Month* magazine writer Maria Samarin:

I was on the beat one night in 1944 when I caught three boys trying to jam the lock on a grocery store near the old Fire Hall on Pitt Street. I walked the boys from Pitt Street to the Police Station where I checked to see whether they had a record.

Samarin wrote that after Parker checked, he kept their names off the blotter: "He explained that he was always careful not to book juveniles who had no prior offenses so as not to give them a police record."

Instead Parker talked to the boys personally until 2 a.m., then telephoned their parents and talked to them, too. As it turned out, one of those boys went on to become a cabinet minister in the Yukon Territory.

Being remembered for Uncle Al's Kids Party was enough for Parker. He got the idea back in 1966. He was sitting at the kitchen table having breakfast. He told a writer for *Windsor This Month* that he could see kids "in pajamas coming into the playground area early in the morning because they had nowhere else to go."

Parker knew most of these kids from the neighborhood, and worried that they might get into trouble. It was then that he asked his wife, Evelyn, what could be done for them. Even in a small way. She suggested a party just before school started in September.

As he told *Windsor This Month* in December 1984, "My wife set about almost at once to prepare the sandwiches, cookies and lemonade for the 24 children who attended our party that first year." As the years went on, the more elaborate the parties got. Dignitaries would show up, and Parker organized parades, and even introduced go-carts.

In time, the idea of holding a party took on a whole new meaning. Parker saw it as a means of teaching children good citizenship and cooperation.

Alton Parker died Feb. 28, 1989.

The Humanitarian
Frank Chauvin

That day in May 1955 is one that Frank Chauvin won't forget. He was finishing up his round of bread deliveries to Riverside homes when he stopped by the Riverside Police Department. Chief Bryce Monaghan had asked him to come by.

"That's when they handed me a gun, a holster, a Sam Browne belt, a pair of pants, and a shirt. And the next day I put these on and I was working for the Riverside Police. Just like that. No training ."

Chauvin, better known to Windsor as a great humanitarian for trucking food, clothing, toys and furniture to the Madonna house in Combermere near Ottawa, and bringing help to the poor in Haiti, laughs about it now.

"I didn't know what I was doing back then. They handed me a set of keys, and put me out on patrol . . . I just hoped and prayed that nothing happened, that I wouldn't get bank robbery on my first day, because I wouldn't know what the hell to do.

"I didn't know anything. I didn't even know there was a Highway Traffic Act, or what the Criminal Code was."

That was policing in the 1950s in Riverside. To some extent, it was no different in Windsor. Frank Chauvin, son of Cliff Chauvin, former

Members of the Riverside Police Department look over a new agreement in the early 1950s. On the left is Bill Docherty, now a developer in Windsor, and one of Frank Chauvin's early police colleagues.
ws.

police officer and councilor in Riverside, had decided he'd had enough of bread deliveries. For years, he had made the rounds around the town with a wagon pulled by a horse.

He was lucky to get the job as a policeman in Riverside, but his father's position on council helped. But even then, hiring practices were according to religion. Chauvin maintains the politicians would alternate in hiring Protestants and Catholics. Because Catholic was next in line, Chauvin was hired. He recalls one constable, a Protestant who, after being hired, converted to Catholicism. It meant the next two officers hired had to be Protestant.

When Chauvin started with the Riverside Police, he joined Bill Docherty, then a police constable, better known now as a major developer in Windsor.

I remember one Christmas we were working together, and Bill said,

'Let's go downtown.' Well, we couldn't leave our area. We were the only (police) car on the road, and once we got past Pilette, we were out of our boundary. And I was just a new cop, and I didn't want to say anything, but I thought, 'What the hell is this guy up to?' And Bill was quiet.

We drove down to Kresge's. Now, it was 6 o'clock, and everything was closed. Bill told me to stay in the car and watch the radio. I thought, 'Hey, is he robbing the place?' Well, in no time, the staff of the place was filing out, and they filled the car with food, and toys, you name it. And Bill didn't tell me what he was doing with all this stuff. I mean, I was just a junior guy.

Well, we drove back, and he didn't say anything. We drove to a house in Riverside . . . There was a family there of eight kids. They didn't have any food in the house, or toys for the kids that Christmas. And the guy wasn't working. Bill had found out about them and decided to do something about it. He told me never to tell anyone about it. I mean we could

Detective Frank Chauvin is presented his award as a Member of the Order of Canada by the Her Excellency Governor General Jeanne Sauvé. ws.

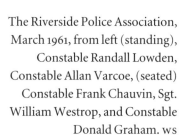

The Riverside Police Association, March 1961, from left (standing), Constable Randall Lowden, Constable Allan Varcoe, (seated) Constable Frank Chauvin, Sgt. William Westrop, and Constable Donald Graham. ws

have lost our jobs for leaving Riverside . . . But he was concerned about that family.

Those first years on the Riverside Force taught Chauvin how to deal properly with people. Policing in those days was far different – in some ways, more humane. "We used to come across some kids and we'd give them a good kick in the butt, and send them home to their parents. We never even made out a report. But, you know, many of them whom I ran into later in life have become prominent citizens here."

Chauvin realizes such down-to-earth practices are no longer tolerated today. But to him, it was a way of meeting people on their terms— without hurting them, without charging them and without sending them through the courts.

"Oh, I used to get fed up with punks on the corner, say at Lauzon and Wyandotte, and I'd pack them in my car and drive them to Pilette and drop them off and tell them to walk back.

"And if I caught them hitchhiking, I'd drive them back to Pilette, and make them do it all over again."

While most policing in Riverside involved traffic violations, Chauvin got his licks. Once he was ganged up upon by youths in Riverside at a dance. The story was played up in the *Windsor Star*, even *Maclean's Magazine*, because it involved a crowd of youths ganging up on a police officer. That was in January 1958.

In 1966, the Riverside Police was absorbed into the Windsor Police

Force, and Chauvin found himself working in the east end. But to make ends meet, he also worked security jobs for the old Hi-Ho ("and fighting all night") or Riverside Arena dances. He contends he preferred not to advance up the ladder too quickly, because he could make more money remaining a constable, and with a large family, he needed part time employment. A job with more responsibility would handicap that activity.

Finally, Chauvin was moved to the special investigations division. In 1975, he was made a detective. The one case he remembers most involved the murder of a young girl in November 1970. He had been on his way home one foggy night, made a wrong turn and ended up on a secluded street. For some reason, he took note of a parked car and part of its licence number. The next morning when he heard a murder had occurred in that vicinity, he gave the information to the department. With that, the police were able to track down the girl's murderer.

Chauvin doesn't know why he had such an "eerie feeling" that night when he spotted that car. He realizes now that had he stopped to investigate, he might have prevented a murder. He remembers noting the time when he passed by that intersection. "It was right about then that this guy had just finished raping the girl." Moments later, when Chauvin had passed by the scene, the man killed her.

In the 1970s, Chauvin began his charity work. He eschewed promotions, preferring to spend every off-duty moment helping the disadvantaged. "I'm satisfied that I could do that, and that I did it."

Windsor Police Auxiliary recruits Glen Skinner and Mary Armaly on the shooting range. 9 March, 1991. WS

The Windsor Police main station downtown: what it looked like after it was first opened. Windsor Police Service Museum.

Police work was his life. He had always wanted to be a policeman, but realized as he got older, there were other priorities he wished to emphasize. That was why he took early retirement. Since then, he has poured himself into working for Canadian Food For Children, for which he is shipping and trucking donations and goods all over the world.

Chauvin realized, too, that one of the draws to being a policeman was that desire to help people. It is still a profession where people can help society. "If you want to take a job to help people, then it's (police work) for you." The unfortunate thing is that not every policeman sees it that way, Chauvin said.

He learned years ago that the best approach – the only decent approach – in dealing with people in police work is to treat them with respect. He made a pact years ago with another detective that whenever they were interrogating youths, they would remind themselves that it was their "own kids" who were sitting there.

"I'd think if that was my kid on the other side of the desk, I'd want him to be treated right . . . I think that attitude paid off."

New facade on Police Headquarters, 1977. J. P. Thomson, Architects.

Windsor Police Service Roll Call
September 1, 1992

Rank	Name	Date of Appt	cadet
Chief of Police	Adkin, J.	23 Oct 61	c
Deputy Chief	Blair, J.	17 Jun 63	c
Superintendent	Dagley, M.	05 Jun 67	
	Burrows, J.	31 Jan 66	c
Staff Inspector	Crichton, B.	15 Jun 57	
	Garswood, J.	19 Nov 56	
	Stannard, G.	01 May 70	
	McGee, R.	29 Nov 65	
Inspector	Thachuk, J.	16 Apr 62	
	Hodgkin, O.	04 Dec 67	
	Chippett, I.	07 Sep 65	
	Gunn, B.	17 Jun 63	c
	Nicholson, J.	12 Apr 65	
	Saunders, R.	04 Jan 66	
	Larkin, K.	13 Dec 65	
	Menzel, G.	29 Nov 65	
	Chevalier, R.	19 May 64	
Staff Sergeant	Oakley, A.	07 Sep 65	
	Klimczak, J.	12 Sep 66	
	Sinnott, M.	20 Nov 66	
	Berekoff, L.	25 Oct 65	
	Biggs, J.	01 May 70	
	Bruynson, E.	04 Jan 66	
	Greenham, B.	22 Jun 69	c
	Westlake, G.	13 Oct 64	
	Snyder, D.	01 May 71	
	Kennedy, R.	16 Oct. 67	
	Jessop, N.	02 Sep 69	
	Grahame, L.	29 Nov 65	
	Wilson, M.	31 Jan 66	
	Ritchie, L.	01 Oct 68	
	McIver, I.	02 Sep 69	
	Lenehan, J.	02 Sep 69	
	Stephens, W.	01 Sep 71	c
	Jee, E.	01 Jun 72	
	Evans, J.	01 Jan 73	
	Stannard, D.	02 Feb 70	c
	Guenot, G.	26 Jul 65	
	Barker, T.	01 May 70	
	Pocock, G.	01 May 70	
	Roberts, D.	01 May 70	c
	Gervais, T.	01 Jul 73	c

Rank	Name	Date of Appt	cadet
Detective	McNorton, E.	01 Jan 73	
	Garrett, R.	01 Jun 63	
	Harris, G.	16 Nov 62	
	Parent, J.	16 Mar 64	
	Monchamp, R.	26 Jul 65	
	Arseneault, D.	13 Dec 65	
	Wiley, D.	17 Feb 64	c
	Workman, D.	01 Feb 63	
	Lozinski, M.	21 Jun 65	
	Seguin, A.	01 Feb 65	
	Berneche, L.	31 Jan 66	
	Powers, K.	01 May 70	
	McIntosh, C.	31 Jan 66	
	Hobbs, M.	31 Jan 66	
	Gilliam, J.	31 Jan 66	
	Clarke, L.	31 Jan 66	
	Wiseman, W.	04 Jan 66	
	Raven, W.	02 Dec 68	c
	Potvin, R.	04 Jan 66	
	Adkin, R.	26 Jul 65	c
	Bondy, K.	02 Mar 69	c
	Wells, A.	26 Jul 65	c
	Kidd, G.	01 Jan 70	
	Garbutt, J.	05 Dec 66	
	Sanders	01 May 73	
	Lester, N.	01 Feb 68	
	Green, R.	01 Jun 72	
	Kelly, M.L.	22 Jun 69	c
	Graber, D.	01 May 71	
	Eve, M.	01 May 70	c
	Lucier, R.	01 May 71	
	Talbot, T.	01 Jan 70	c
	Hartigan, R.	01 Oct 68	
	Hardstone, D.	01 May 70	
	Menard, B.	02 Jul 75	
	Paterson, J.	01 Jun 72	
	White, J.	20 Jun 66	
	Cowper, R.	01 Jan 73	
	Ronson, L.	01 Jan 70	
	Ing., D.	05 Dec 66	
	Renaud, G.	07 Sep 76	c
	Lovell, C.	02 Jan 76	c
	Ducharme, D.	01 Jul 73	
Sergeant	Wirrell, J.	01 May 62	
	Skinner, L.	03 Jan 62	
	Purton, D.	01 Apr 65	
	McKnight, L.	29 Nov 65	
	Grail, L.	01 Jun 64	
	Mercer, R.	24 May 66	
	McCullough, P.	01 Jan 70	
	Delmore, C.	01 Oct 68	

Name	Date	c	Unit	Name	Date	c
Woods, D.	01 Jan 72			Mawhinney, J.	01 Jan 70	
Mortimore, R.	01 May 71		(Courts)	Jenkins, G.	01 May 70	
Hussey, R.	02 Dec 68			Atkinson, J.	14 May 70	
Briese, L.	01 Sep 62		(Courts)	Gammon, D.	01 May 71	
Nichols, R.	29 Nov 65		(Courts)	Speranza, C.	01 Jan 72	
Fortier, T.	02 Dec 68	c		Kelly, M.D.	03 Jan 71	c
Sampson, D.	01 Jan 70		(Courts)	Haines, K.	03 Jan 71	c
Smith, G.	01 Jun 74	c		Stewart, C.	01 Jun 72	
McPhee, G.	01 Jul 73		(Traffic)	Oleynik, J.	01 Jun 72	
Smith, P.	01 Oct 76			Holden, E.	01 Jun 72	
Lenehan, M.	01 Jul 73			Charlton, J.	02 Jul 71	c
Monteleone, J.	02 Mar 69	c		Madden, M.	15 Jan 73	
Rodd, T.	01 Jun 72	c		Rundle, J.	01 Apr 73	
McFarland, K.	17 Nov 74	c		Holman, K.	01 Oct 71	c
Stephens, M.	01 Nov 73			Doidge, D.	15 Jan 74	
MacMillan, R.	02 Jul 75		(Traffic)	Wiley, W.	15 Jan 74	
Pickford, d.	20 Mar 77			Koekstat, K.	01 Jun 74	
Mombourquette, P.	02 Jan 76			Scheirich, N.	20 Nov 72	c
Gill, R.	01 Jun 72	c		Moor, J.	01 Jul 73	c
Zerbin, D.	14 Aug 67	c		Hill, R.	01 Jun 74	c
Reid, E.	01 May 60	c		George, D.	17 Nov 74	c
Brown, A.	02 Jan 76	c		Jolie, G.	19 Dec 76	
Nawalany, P.	02 Jul 75			MacKenzie, M.	19 Dec 76	
Rettig, R.	02 Jul 75			Ouellette, G.	02 Jan 76	c
Zajac, B.	01 May 70		(Traffic)	Skuza, J.	02 Jan 76	c
Gibbon, P.	02 Sep 69			Gagnon, E.	06 Sep 77	c
Lemon, P.	01 Jun 72			Stannard, M.	96 Sep 77	c
Stevenson, J.	01 Sep 72	c		Pellett, G.	19 Dec 77	c
Rossell, D.	01 Aug 78			Trudell, K.	16 Jul 78	c
Forbes, R.	19 Dec 76			Hall, D.	08 Jul 79	
				Perpich, D.	06 Nov 79	
				Brannagan, J.	27 Jan 80	
				Kelly, M.P.	27 Jan 80	

Constables

Unit	Name	Date	c	Name	Date	c
				Strilchuck, D.	01 May 79	c
(Courts)	Curtis, H.	04 Mar 63		Prior, P.	01 May 79	c
	Bickford, H.	16 Mar 64		Leblanc, P.	01 May 79	c
	Bishop, P.	02 Dec 63	c	Everingham, B.	01 Oct 80	
	Charlton, M.	01 Apr 65		Boots, L.	01 Oct 80	
	Copland, T.	05 Jul 65	c	Smith, J.	01 Oct 80	
	Scratch, B.	09 Aug 65	c	Baldwin, J.	01 May 79	c
(Bylaws)	DeJong, H.	04 Jan 66		Scott, D.	01 May 79	c
(Traffic)	Hood, W.	31 Jan 66		Fontaine, M.	08 Jul 79	c
(Courts)	Zan, G.	31 Jan 66		Murphy, T.	27 Jan 80	c
(Courts)	Oberemok, J.	31 Jan 66		Stibbard, W.	20 Apr 80	c
(Courts)	Pomeroy, G.	31 Jan 66		Steiner, G.	20 Apr 80	c
(Traffic)	Eastlake, L.	31 Jan 66		Kowal, S.	20 Apr 80	c
(Courts)	Sheffiel, D.	07 Feb 66		Rettig, T.	20 Apr 80	c
	Curtis, M.	04 Jan 66	c	Sarkis, W.	01 Oct 80	c
	McGeouch, D.	29 Aug 66	c	Crough, K.	01 Oct 80	c
(Traffic)	Seguin, P.	11 Sep 67	c	Martin, W.	13 Jul 81	c
	Silivria, W.	27 Apr 69		Drake, E.	13 Jul 81	c
	Miller, D.	12 May 69		Brown, M.	07 Sep 76	
	Bulmer, R.	02 Sep 69	(Traffic)	Sinnott, P.	20 Mar 77	

	Green, W.	20 May 86			Lane, B.	12 Jan 87	c
	Thompson, A.	28 Jun 82	c		Lamarche, S.	12 Jan 87	c
	Bachmeier, J.	08 Sep 82	c		Sekela, M.	12 Jan 87	c
	Richards, J.	28 Jun 82	c		Maodus, N.	12 Jan 87	c
	Rieti, U.	28 Jun 82	c		Kigar, D.	05 Oct 87	c
	Meloche, G.	07 Sep 82	c		Wilson, S.	05 Oct 87	c
	Robinson, M.	02 Aug 83	c		Van Buskirk, D.	05 Oct 87	c
(Traffic)	Fasan, R.	02 Aug 83	c		Denonville, M.	05 Oct 87	c
	Labute, R.	02 Aug 83	c		Dickson, S.	05 Oct 87	c
	Comelli, M.	02 Aug 83	c		Facciolo, R.	25 Jul 88	
	Yearley, G.	02 Aug 83	c		McLaughlin, B.	05 Oct 87	c
	Gervais, G.	02 Aug 83	c		Couloufis, P.	05 Oct 87	c
(Traffic)	Cassady, D.	02 Aug 83	c		Spratt, R.	05 Oct 87	c
	Byrd, S.	02 Aug 83	c		Fortune, M.	05 Oct 87	c
	Adams, A.	14 May 84	c		Giampuzzi, V.	05 Oct 87	c
	Shannon, D.	14 May 84	c		Providenti, F.	05 Oct 87	c
	DeHoop, J.	14 May 84	c		Reid, T.	05 Oct 87	c
	Ducharme, M. D.	14 May 84	c		Mosher, P.	05 Oct 87	c
	Hill, B.	03 Jul 84	c		Tomen, J.	05 Oct 87	c
	Turner, R.	03 Jul 84	c		Verkoeyen, J.	04 Jan 88	c
	Loebach, G.	03 Jul 84	c		Hartlieb, T. Jr.	04 Jan 88	c
	Frederick, A.	03 Jul 84	c		Kiteley, R.	04 Jan 88	c
	Crowley, T.	03 Jul 84	c		Mediratta, S.	04 Jan 88	c
	Pizzicaroli, A.	03 Jul 84	c		Lucier, J.	04 Jan 88	c
	Beer, M.	03 Jul 84	c		Balkwill, C.	04 Jan 88	c
	Denomme, M.	03 Jul 84	c		Szalay, T.	04 Jan 88	c
	Jacobs, L.	15 Oct 84	c		Vidler, G.	25 Jul 88	c
	Virtue, N.	15 Oct 84	c		Dunn, J.	25 Jul 88	c
	Killops, E.	15 Jul 85	c		St. Louis, J.	25 Jul 88	c
	Siddle, J.	15 Jul 85	c		Nohra, E.	25 Jul 88	c
	Virban, J.	15 Jul 85	c		Libby, C.	04 Jan 88	c
	Hool, J.	15 Jul 85	c		NcCann, K.	25 Jul 88	c
	Bridgeman, P.	15 Jul 85	c		Marion, F.	25 Jul 88	c
	Power, V.	15 Jul 85	c		Jibinville, J.	25 Jul 88	c
	Keane, P.	15 Jul 85	c		Marentette, M.	25 Jul 88	c
	Croley, P.	15 Jul 85	c		MacDonald, S.	25 Jul 88	c
	Jean, P.	15 Jul 85	c		Ducharme, M. Jos.	25 Jul 88	c
	McCulloch, T.	15 Jul 85	c		Hickey, E.	24 Jul 88	c
	Jones, R.	01 Dec 85	c		Cote, R.	25 Jul 88	c
(Traffic)	Sharron, T.	01 Dec 85	c		Robertson, M.	25 Jul 88	c
	Lamarre, G.	20 May 86	c		Spadafora, B.	25 Jul 88	c
	Ritchie, S.	20 May 86	c		Lefler, D.	17 Oct 88	c
	Doman, C.	20 May 86	c		DeMarchi, D.	06 Mar 89	c
	Corey, R.	20 May 86	c		Klyn, T.	08 May 89	c
	Severin, F.	20 May 86	c		Cockburn, J.	08 May 89	c
	Rebkowec, C.	07 Jul 86	c		Suthers, J.	16 Jul 89	c
	Levesque, G.	07 Jul 86	c		Diluca, R.	16 Jul 89	c
	Boyle, J.	07 Jul 86	c		Lalonde, M.	16 Jul 89	c
	Symons, K.	20 May 86	c		White, P.	16 Jul 89	c
	Cowper, D.	12 Jan 87	c		Sansburn, I.	16 Jul 89	c
	Stock, M.	12 Jan 87	c		Renaud, Gary	06 Mar 89	c
	Coughlin, J.	12 Jan 87	c		Allison, J.	16 Jul 89	c

	Moxley, A.	16 Jul 89	c
	Quiding, M.	02 Jan 90	c
	Gillis, A.	02 Jan 90	c
	Belanger, J.	02 Jan 90	c
	Lee, K.	02 Jan 90	c
	D'Asti, M.	02 Jan 90	c
	Gazdig, B.	02 Jan 90	c
	McGhee, M.	02 Jan 90	c
	Markett, T.	02 Jan 90	c
	Cox, T.	02 Jan 90	c
	Beauchamp, R.	02 Jan 90	c
	Lepine, J.	02 Jan 90	c
	Sequeira, K.	02 Jan 90	c
	Landry, M.	02 Jan 90	c
	Westenberg, J.	02 Jan 90	c
	Dupuis, C.	02 Jan 90	c
	Lebert, M.	02 Jan 90	c
	Jones, M.	02 Jan 90	c
	Booze, M.	02 Jan 90	c
	Garro, A.	07 Jan 91	c
	Hope, L.	07 Jan 91	c
	Leclair, R.	07 Jan 91	c
	Dosant, W.	07 Jan 91	c
	Iler, C.	07 Jan 91	c
	Suich, D.	07 Jan 91	c
	Kovacic, J.	07 Jan 91	c
	Ajersch, J.	07 Jan 91	c
	Malolepszy, R.	07 Jan 91	c
	Coughlin, A.	07 Jan 91	c
	Mailloux, J.	07 Jan 91	c
	Chemello, G.	07 Jan 91	c
	Evans, M.	26 Feb 90	SPC
	Bender, S.	07 Oct 91	c
	Klimczak, L.	07 Oct 91	c
	Wortley, S.	07 Oct 91	c
	Summers, J.S.	07 Oct 91	c
C.I.U.	Glen, W.	01 Jun 64	
	Gazdig, J.	25 Oct 65	
	Brooks, D.	07 Feb 66	
	Beckett, W.	15 Jul 68	
	Haines, G.	06 Sep 77	c
	Parent, J.	16 Jul 78	c
	Bordi, S.	01 May 79	c
	Corriveau, G.	28 Jun 82	c
S.I.B.	Thompson, R.	07 Sep 65	
	Burko, G.	05 Dec 66	c
	Beecroft, W.	15 Jul 68	c
	Hartlieb, T. Sr.	01 May 70	
	Gungle, K.	03 Jan 31	c
	Luxford, K.	01 Jun 72	c

	Hayes, T.	01 Nov 72	c
	Walker, J.	01 Nov 73	
	Purdy, G.	02 Jul 75	
	Ludschuweit, A.	02 Jan 76	
	McVitty, M.	19 Dec 76	
	Dynan, R.	19 Dec 76	
	Severin, J.	02 Jul 75	c
	Levack, G.	02 Jan 76	c
	Wilson, G.	16 Jul 78	c
Admin.			
(Range)	Brown, D.	04 Jan 66	
(Comm.Srv)	Cincurak, S.	02 Jul 75	
(Training)	Mason, R.	27 Jan 80	
(Comm.Srv)	Laporte, M.	27 Jan 80	
(Comm.Srv)	McQuire, J.	01 May 79	c
(Comm.Srv)	Belanger, K.	01 Oct 80	c
Ident.	Skreptak, M.	01 Jun 72	
	Zalisko, M.	01 Jul 73	c
	Hooper, P.	01 Nov 73	c
	Halpert, W.	27 Jan 80	
	Donnelly, W.	20 May 86	c
	Dunmore, G.	12 Jan 87	c
B & E	Whitesell, W.	01 Jun 72	
Domest. Violence	Taylor, L.	02 Jul 75	
Drug Squad	Parsons, W.	02 Jan 76	c
	Williams, D.	01 Oct 80	c
	Burkoski, N.	01 Oct 80	c
	Langlois, M.	02 Aug 83	c
	Lugosi, J.	01 Dec 85	c
	McMillan, K.	12 Jan 87	c
	Bissonnette, C.	05 Oct 87	c
Police c			
	Moon, R.	30 Dec 91	
	Delmonte, L.	30 Dec 91	
	Atkinson, J.	30 Dec 91	
	McCormick, S.	30 Dec 91	
	Shannon, M.	30 Dec 91	
	Williams, G.	30 Dec 91	
	McCubbin, D.	30 Dec 91	
	Middleton-Wilson, J.	30 Dec 91	
	Quinn, M.	30 Dec 91	
	Hebert, J.	30 Dec 91	
	Farrand, J.	30 Dec 91	
	Haidy, M.	30 Dec 91	

	McKenzie, A.		30 Dec 91
	Tetrault, G.		30 Dec 91
	Lamont, S.		30 Dec 91
	Jaworiwsky, S.		30 Dec 91
	Drago, R.		30 Dec 91
	Souchuk, J.		30 Dec 91
	Fortune, K.		30 Dec 91
	Riberdy, L.		30 Dec 91

Civilian Staff

Grade	Branch	Name	Date
1.	C.R.	Koutros, M.	03 Jun 90
	C.R.	Merritt, S.	03 Feb 92
2.	C.R.	Lemon, B.	07 Apr 91
	C.R.	Torti, L.	16 Apr 92
3.	INV.	Bertoni, M.	06 Apr 92
4.	C.R.	Forbes, A.	21 Apr 86
	ADMIN.	Denes, A.	21 Mar 88
	C.R.	Girard, E.	02 Oct 89
	C.R.	Stradiotto, R.	02 Oct 89
	C.R.	Gray, S.	07 Jan 91
	PAT.	Bagnarol, M.	05 Aug 90
5.	C.R.	Little, V.	21 Mar 88
	PAT.CTS.	Moroun, J.	06 Feb 89
	ADMIN.	Forbis, P.	02 Oct 89
	ADMIN.	Bachmeier, M.	09 Oct 84
	INV.	Whited, E.	01 May 90
	INV.	Racicot, P.	01 May 90
	INV.	Papineau, M.	02 Jan 90
	INV.	McCall, D.	11 Nov 90
	PAT.CTS.	Brosseau, L.	21 Apr 81
6.	PAT.	Lantz, C.	01 Feb 72
	ADMIN.	Haines, J.	23 May 72
	C.R.	Denomme, R.	12 Jul 76
	C.R.	Donnelly, N.	01 Aug 73
	C.R.	Meyers, M.	21 Nov 88
	C.R.	Chaborek, B.	01 May 90
	C.R.	Miranda, T.	02 Oct 89
	INV.	Yiannou, K.	02 Apr 73
	INV.	Nawalany, R.	01 Dec 69
	C.R.	Hole, C.	01 May 90
	ADMIN.	Dennis, E.J.	01 Jan 91
	C.R.	Charlton, A.	30 Jan 91
	C.R.	Pinell, I.	09 Jun 91
7.	C.R.	Onuch, B.	02 Jul 68
	PAT.	Marino, C.	01 Aug 73
	PAT.CTS.	Uljarevic, J.	04 Jan 81
	C.R.	Parent, A.	11 Mar 74
	C.R.	Shaw, D.	21 Nov 88
	ADMIN.	Nemeth, B.	05 Nov 79
	ADMIN.	Louis, B.	17 Sep 84
	C.R.	Hurst, D.	01 May 90
	ADMIN.	Firby, M.	02 Oct 89
8.	ADMIN.	Rivard, R.	02 Dec 69
	C.R.	Robinson, L.	03 Jul 72
	C.R.	Rusnak, L.	01 Apr 74
	C.R.	Severin, S.	23 Mar 80
	C.R.	Morgan, D.	21 Apr 81
	C.R.	Edmondson, T.	15 Nov 82
	C.R.	Wilkes, J.	21 Apr 91
	C.R.	Keyeux, S.	03 Feb 91
	ADMIN.	McMullen, M.	26 May 88
	C.R.	Bondy, D.	30 Oct 78
9.	ADMIN.	Turner, T.	21 Apr 69
	PAT.	Shulman, D.	26 Feb 90
	PAT.	Minto, G.	26 Feb 90
	PAT.	Bennett, S.	26 Feb 90
	PAT.	Windsor, J.	26 Feb 90
	PAT.	Butler, D.	10 Jun 90
	PAT.	Timm, B.	26 Feb 90
10.	INV.	Wells, A.	21 Apr 69
	PAT.	Lamoure, J.	26 Feb 90
	PAT.	Mitchell, K.	26 Feb 90
	PAT.	Zold, D.	26 Feb 90
	PAT.	Moore, R.	26 Feb 90
	PAT.	Greenway, J.	08 Apr 90
	PAT.	Campeau, A.	26 Feb 90
	ADMIN.	Mortimore, E.	12 Nov 75
	PAT.	Forde, R.	29 Sep 91
	PAT.	Gratton, P.	23 Mar 92
	C.R.	Vancoughnett, S.	01 Aug 73
11.	INV.	Evans, C.	01 Dec 77
	PAT (COM)	Dutkewich, K.	02 Jan 79
	PAT (COM)	Sheffiel, D.	02 Jul 79
	PAT (COM)	Harris, M.	05 Nov 79
	INV.	Heimann, Donna	23 Mar 80
	PAT (COM)	Zinyk, N.	23 Mar 80
	PAT (COM)	Powers, L.	05 Aug 86
	PAT (COM)	White, J.	30 Jan 84
	PAT (COM)	Webster, J.	12 Apr 85
	PAT (COM)	Lanoue, M.	14 Apr 86

PAT (COM)	Pegg, C.	05 Aug 86	
PAT (COM)	Webster, M.	05 Aug 86	
PAT (COM)	Armstrong-Rice, C.	14 Oct 86	
PAT (COM)	Gillis, D.	27 Apr 87	
PAT (COM)	Foreman, L.	09 May 88	
PAT (COM)	Ingersoll, J.	21 Mar 88	
PAT (COM)	Shamblaw, B.	20 Jun 88	
PAT (COM)	Marek, L.	18 Jan 89	
PAT (COM)	Smith, M.	21 Feb 83	
PAT (COM)	Pszczonak, J.	07 Jan 90	
PAT (COM)	Wright, A.	03 Jan 89	
C.R.	Johnson, J.	20 Sep 78	
PAT.	Sivell, K.	27 May 74	
PAT.	Armaly, P.	26 Feb 90	
PAT (COM)	Fitzgerald, P.	15 Jul 90	
PAT (COM)	Donnelly, K.	15 Jul 90	
PAT (COM)	Chaborek, D.	15 Jul 90	
PAT (COM)	Pelletier, E.	15 Jul 90	
PAT (COM)	Lenehan, S.	15 Jul 90	
PAT (COM)	Elsido, C.	29 Mar 92	
PAT (COM)	Shadd, S.	02 Aug 92	

12.	PAT (COM)	Farley, J.	30 Apr 79
	PAT (COM)	Kourelias, C.	30 Apr 79
	PAT (COM)	Taylor, C.	02 Jan 79
	PAT (COM)	Vetor, S.	23 Mar 80
	ADMIN.	Kujbida, M.	28 May 89
	PAT (COM)	Newton, A.	19 Jul 82

13.	ADMIN.	Stewart, G	08 May 89
	ADMIN.	Synnott, N.	25 Feb 91
	ADMIN.	Gagnon, S.	01 Sep 79

14.	ADMIN.	Kelly, P.	14 Jun 79

15.	ADMIN.	Horrobin, B.	17 Jul 89

16.	ADMIN.	Mcmullen, S.	15 May 72
	ADMIN.	Heimann, D.	07 Apr 86
	ADMIN.	Solan, M.	05 May 86

Biographical Notes

C. H. Gervais is best known for his book *The Rumrunners*, a history of Prohibition in Canada. He is a journalist, poet, playwright and historian. Gervais, the author of nine books of poetry, two plays, is the recipient of numerous journalism awards. In 1990, he was runner-up for the Milton Acorn Memorial People's Poetry Award. Gervais is currently Book Editor at *The Windsor Star*.

    Mary E. Baruth, a graduate in history from the University of Windsor, is the curator at the Backus Historical Complex for the Long Point Region Conservation Authority. She recently completed the certificate in museum studies program from the Ontario Museum Association. **G. Mark Walsh** is a graduate in history from the University of Windsor, and studied archival administration at Wayne State University. He is currently Windsor's municipal archivist, and a member of the Academy of Certified Archivists.

Selected Bibliography

Bartlet, Alexander, *The Diaries of Alexander Bartlet,* unpublished, The Municipal Archives and the University of Windsor.

Callwood, June, *Portrait of Canada,* Doubleday, 1981

Engelmann, Larry, *Intemperance, The Lost War Against Liquor,* Free Press, Macmillan, 1979.

Gervais, C. H., *The Rumrunners: A Prohibition Scrapbook,* Firefly, 1980.

MacDonald, Cheryl, "Gilbert McMicken, Spymaster, Canada's Secret   Police," *The Beaver,* June-July 1991.

Morrison, Neil, F., *Garden Gateway to Canada,* Herald Press, 1954.

Morgan, Carl, *Birth Of A City,* 1991.

Neal, Frederick, *The Township of Sandwich,* The Essex County Historical Society and The Windsor Public Library Board, 1979.

Stenning, Philip, C., *Legal Status of Police,* Law Reform Commission of Canada, 1981.